Prologue

I am Zoe, Dryad of Crete. Yes, I live in a tree, my ears are pointed, my hair is green (I refuse to disclose my age). But the story I wish to tell is less of me than of Silver Bells, the last of the Minotaurs (except his nephew Eunostos, still a child); and the Humans, Lordon and Hora, who invaded my Country but not to conquer or kill. (Lordon, bless him, will help me to tell my tale, for he knows the human heart.)

I must also describe the Sphinx, the monster from Egypt, though the tiniest thought of her is like a thunderous wave, which churns you and chokes you and bruises your face with coral; and threatens to drown.

A good listener never interrupts.

G.Barr

CRY SILVER BELLS

**Thomas
Burnett
Swann**

Illustrated by
George Barr

DAW BOOKS, INC.

DONALD A. WOLLHEIM, PUBLISHER

1301 Avenue of the Americas
New York, N.Y.   10019

Cover art by George Barr.

Acknowledgments: "The Star Birds" is reprinted with the permission of the long-defunct *New York Herald-Tribune*; "The Snow and the Seed" with the permission of the *New York Times*.

DEDICATION

To Edith,
my beloved niece

FIRST PRINTING, DECEMBER 1977

1 2 3 4 5 6 7 8 9

PRINTED IN U.S.A.

Chapter One

Lordon

"Poppies," I said. "The city looks like a swirl of poppies."

"Men," retorted my cousin Hora, her eyes enlarging with expectation. "Stalwart young men in loin cloths. Older men with money bags at their waists. Being a courtesan is the best of occupations. You are paid to please, but the pleasing can be delightful as well as profitable. If the men are young or rich."

"You know you can't see that far. They just look like bluebottle flies crawling about in search of mates. Why, you can't even make out the nets of those fishermen in their little boats."

"No, but I can imagine."

"And how about *me?* Do I look properly roguish?" I cocked an eye and attempted a suitable leer.

"You look like a pirate," she said. Hora was tactful. I looked like a pauper in my tattered loin cloth and my old, scruffed sandals from Egypt. Oh, for a ring, an armlet, a pectoral. . . . To be a successful thief, you must either appear to be rich or simple-minded and then the people will trust you.

5

Hora and I, exiled from Egypt after the unfortunate incident of my arrest for theft and assault, had sailed to Crete to ply our twin trades of thievery and prostitution.

"Poppies," I repeated. Blue and red, blue and red. . . . No other colors obtruded into the rock-island city of Pseira, except for the coconut palms which swayed like enormous stems among the poppies. Titanic flowers in a living mound, the building seemed, the oblong houses, the local palace, the marketplace and the ships with their colored sails. Red bulbous columns like upended trees, supporting roofs abristle with furniture—stone couches shaded by flaxen parasols; lustral basins; urns of sun-baked clay. Blue, rounded facades. Staircases spiraling into the waveless sea. No city walls, of course. Ships were the walls of Crete, and instead of jetties or buoys, the sandy, surrounding beach was fingered with berths whose separations were rows of driftwood and seashells. "Poppies *and* riches. I think we are—Hora, the sun is gone! And there—a black cloud. Are we in for a storm?"

A storm in truth, but worse than wind and rain. . . .

Thus did the Harpies attack an unarmed merchant ship. The sailors brandished oars in place of swords, but onyx-hard talons snatched them from the oarsmen and splintered them over our heads. A rent and the sail fell in shreds. A blow and the mast was a falling tree. Hora seized my arm but not out of fear. Older, she liked to protect me, and she was unshakeable under attack. She hurried me into the deck house and fastened the leathern hanging which served for a door.

"I don't even have a dagger," I said. "They took it from me in Egypt."

"Maybe they won't come looking for us in here."

They did not come through the door; they came through the wall of bundled papyrus reeds; one, at least.

"Pimp and thief though I am, dear Hermes, be with me now!" I prayed. "I have stolen nothing from *her!*"

She was not a woman except for her face. She stared at me through the rent she had clawed in the wall, and her hands indeed were talons, and twisted like driftwood old from the sea. I caught a glimpse of wings, black, leathery, bat-like, and feathers around her flanks. The stench of her was worse than a rotting squid.

Only her face seemed human. The face of a queen who has sacrificed her husband to insure fertility for the fields. Hair, brows, scowl: implacable black. But skin as white as a nautilus bleached in the sun. The Harpies inhabit caves and only dare the light in search of food or murder, or to visit their friends, the Sphinxes (hateful word!), across the sea. A Harpy is stupid and cruel. A Sphinx is canny and cruel. There is something of woman distorted in each of them, and the Sphinx, it is thought by some, can metamorphose herself into human form, and then she is known as a Lamia, and she lures a man in order to drink his blood.

But Lamias were a possibility; the truth was a Harpy clawing the wall.

"The Lady is dead," she spat.

It was not a time to inquire what lady or why a Harpy would care for any lady. It was a time to prevent her from enlarging the hole and springing into the cabin and at my throat. (Hora was searching frantically for a makeshift weapon.) I seized a lamp and sloshed the olive oil in her face. She shrieked— the oil was hot—and rubbed her eyes and forgot for the moment her mission: that is to say, the imminent death of a blond and inoffensive youth of seventeen whose only transgression had been to crack an occasional skull and steal an occasional money bag, which he graciously shared with his cousin, the courtesan, in those difficult times when her lovers were insufficient for her wants (and when it suited his whim). I liked my work. A pirate at heart, I performed my petty thefts with the hope of amassing a fortune and buying a ship with a Gorgon prow and staring, lidless eyes, and *then* let the virgins look to their maiden heads!

Swat! Hora had found her weapon, the lid of a cedar chest, and the Harpy reeled into sleep (at least I think it was sleep; she never closed her eyes; they never lost their hate).

"Lordon," cried Hora, clutching my arm. She was rarely ruffled, my cousin; control was the mark of her trade. But danger to me aroused her to action. "Did she hurt you, that blackfeathered bitch?"

"Not a scratch."

"But we've hit something—shoals, do you think? And what on earth is that!"

The ship gave a sudden lurch and began to sink; water rose murkily around our feet; we made for the door in time to find ourselves afloat on a tranquil sea with our ship unaccountably sinking beside us. Chest, lidless and overturned . . . cedar table . . . hammocks . . . oars . . . spars . . . griffin figurehead . . . littered the surface as if there had been a storm. Harpies circled above us, cawing like gulls, swooping to claw at a sailor's eyes or shove him under the water. Three of the creatures were dragging a sailor into the air and licking his blood as they flew.

"The chest," breathed Hora. "Under it." We clung to the underside of the chest, breathing the air trapped above us. The chest, overturned, had lost its store and become both a shield and a buoy.

"Well," said Hora, her whisper multiplied in our cramped asylum. 'We've seen worse times, cousin dear. I expect we shall survive. We can swim to Pseira. After those Harpies depart."

"They've departed," I said, peering from under the chest. I sniffed the air. "Except their stench. As swiftly as they came. They seem to live on a rock over there beyond the town. But the sea's been calm. We couldn't have hit a wreck. Why did we sink?"

"It wasn't a natural wreck. Harpies can swim, you know. They simply dragged us, ship and all, under the surface. First they clawed holes in the hull to let in the water."

9

"Harpies this close to Crete? I thought the island was civilized."

"So is Lower Egypt, but it still has its Sphinxes."

"Marguerite, you were never to say that word. We promised each other, you know."

"I *will* say the word Sphinx. Now we are safe from them and we don't have to move from place to place and hide."

"Hush, Marguerite!"

Her bravado faded into a pitiful gasp. "You're right. No one is ever safe from a Sphinx, and I tempted the gods with my foolish claim. Anyway, Crete is only settled along the coast. Inland, there are forests and mountains nobody has ever seen. There are Satyrs and Minotaurs and Panisci and Centaurs and Harpies, I have no doubt."

"And Gorgons perhaps? We'll stick to the coast," I said, shoving the chest from over our heads and onto its bottom and making it into a raft. "With your yellow hair, your trade should flourish among these black-haired folk."

"Yes," she sighed. "As it did in Egypt until you hit a prince. We didn't even need the money."

"I just didn't hit him hard enough. He came to and recognized me. And as for the money, he hadn't paid, you recall. Besides, I fancied his dagger with chrysolite in its hilt, and you'd been spending *everything* on yourself. Here. Let me help you off with your slippers." Already I had discarded my sandals. The water felt cool and clean to my unencumbered feet.

10

"I'm not a spring peahen, you know. *Twenty* last month. At twenty-five, one is over the mountain in my profession. Already I am spending a fortune on kohl, carmine, galena, myrrh, to say nothing of mirrors—"

"Eleven? Or is it twelve?"

"I weary of looking into the same bronze. Mirrors and tweezers and, of course, robes. You know I could never stand parsimony."

"You haven't been parsimonious with yourself since your first assignation."

My words were lost in a gurgle as she shoved me under the water.

I rose with a sputter and splashed her in the face. Hora and I were cronies even before we were cousins. "It *is* a bit of a Satyr," I laughed. I had learned the phrase on the ship from one of the sailors. "Satyr" meant "escapade." "We've never been shipwrecked by Harpies before. And think of all the men—and purses—that wait on the shore. But here. Let me wipe your face."

"Ho there," cried a mullet-faced fisherman from an open boat with two red eyes on its prow. "Need a ride? Saw the whole thing. Them Harpies can be real bitches. Keep to the rocks, usually, but somethin' 'pears to have riled them." His head had the look of having been squashed by Charybdis. The nose did a lamentable job of separating protrusive eyes.

With the help of the fisherman and his crew of one, a cross-eyed child of tender years—fifteen at the most —we clambered into the boat and cleared a space

11

amidst nets, a wriggle of squids, and the smell of yesterday's catch. The child gaped at Hora and dropped his oar.

"Am I still a mess?" she whispered to me.

Cleansed of kohl and carmine, she looked like a fine lady who had lost her ship but not her dignity. Her skin was conch-shell pink, her eyes so blue that kohl would seem an affront.

"Adequate."

"But I need to look *plyful*." Then to the fisherman: "Sir, we are deeply in your debt. We have lost everything. How can we ever repay you?"

"You know very well how you can repay him," I whispered. She stifled me with a furtive slap.

"Got a good catch. Don't need pay." He pointed to the bustling rock of Pseira. "There's my town. Island, really. Special berth for my boat. Boy and me lives in a cave. Not fit for a fine lady like you. Show you to the caravanserai, and the folk 'ull doubtless see to your wants."

"I doubt it," I said, but the child responded with a squinty glare and turned to examine Hora. He wore a knife with a cypress hilt and a blade which had doubtless gutted many a fish.

She had started to make arrangements for our arrival.

Egyptian ladies never bare their breasts; it is only the slave girls who frolic naked in palace corridors. But the Cretan custom of open bodices and painted nipples was universally known, often condemned, secretly admired by the whole of the civilized world.

Somehow, Hora had removed her bodice. Her breasts, even unpainted, were a double wonderment.

"Two moons," said the child, with the tone of an oracle. "Harvest at that."

For once I agreed with him.

" 'Tis a rare catch we've made today, boy," said his father. "Aphrodite from the foam!" He poled his boat into one of the fingered berths.

"Wish we had drowned her friend," mumbled the child. I dealt him a secret kick and gave his father my sweetest smile.

The town was a miracle of controlled spontaneity. It was as if the flower-like buildings had grown in their own fashion and not been planted in neat, Egyptian-style rows. But the fashion suited the place, for a rounded island needed rounded houses, where the mainland cities crouched in rectangular buildings, roughly the shape of Crete. Now in truth we could see the inhabitants, the ladies in purple, bell-shaped skirts like inverted violets (for the murex dye is much in demand for garments); daisies too, since saffron dyes were imported along with tin, gold, papyrus, and ostrich eggs from Egypt, Libya, and other adjacent lands. And the breasts—well, they winked and teased in the sun, and to enclose them would have been like caging a rare bird.

"I think," whispered Hora, "that we have been cast into—what do the Achaeans call it?—Elysium. I have never seen such splendid men." Our parents had come to Egypt from Mycenae, the proudest Achaean city; thus our golden hair among a dark-haired folk.

If the women flaunted their breasts, the men displayed their thighs. Their loin cloths at most were afterthoughts. Clothes to a Cretan were a convenience against a change in the weather, an adornment which emphasized their natural endowments, never a necessity, never a modesty. He liked his world, whether sea, land, or air; he did not like a separation of cloth. They were a small, trim race, brown-skinned from the sun, but lighter as well as smaller than Egyptians. The ladies had carefully teased their hair into ringlets over their foreheads and ears; the men had drawn their hair behind their heads and caught it in leather fillets. Both men and women walked in the pride of their beauty, and satisfaction beamed from their faces.

The fisherman pointed the way to the caravanserai: "May the Goddess shower you with gifts."

"Already has," said the child, meaning Hora, excluding me. (Wretched urchin, might his eyes become *double*-crossed.)

We entered a gate which was flanked with squat limestone griffins, and found before us a lustral basin where we sat on projecting slabs and bathed our feet. The coconut palms above us rustled duskily in the dying sun, for twilight had started its swift descent. Beyond us loomed a maze of small, two- and three-story octagons of brick, faced with limestone and painted a cobalt blue which glittered even in the lessening light.

"Cousin dear," she said. "Do you think they will put us up for the night without pay? The thought of plying, for once, is intolerable to me. Even to be plied. I could sleep through two cockcrow times."

As a rule, Hora required a minimum of sleep. But after our mishap, how could she work her trade (and she worked with a conscientiousness which her lovers —four or five hundred, I forget the count—found to be irresistible)? If payment were needed, my nimble fingers could find the wherewithal. (In fact the cross-eyed child was missing his dagger.)

Voices, soft, insinuating, surmounted the rustle of palms. Ladies in flounced skirts, invariably accompanied by men, wafted out of the octagons. Was every one young on Crete except for the fisherman? Did everyone have a lover or a spouse? Perhaps a stray young girl would wander across my path. . . . Perhaps a stray young woman, ripe with maturity. . . . Perhaps an older woman, mindful of youth's sweet ways. . . .

A young man approached us with purposeful steps and an air of ownership. "My name is Talos. This is my inn." He was small and trim and his face had the look of having been treated and polished like an expensive saddle. If he was leathery from his trade, at least the leather was fine. He wore a phallus sheath and a bronze belt—and I started to feel overdressed in my topless Egyptian tunic which reached to my knees.

"We have heard of a ship attacked by Harpies. Are you perhaps its survivors?"

Hora sighed and gave him a soulful gaze. Dusk had yielded to dark. Newly lit torches of pine illuminated her face, the rubicund skin, the full cheeks, the lips which were red without the deceit of carmine. She made me think of a mulberry tree whose branches were laden with fruit. Though frequently plucked, she always flaunted a crop. Her eyes did not need kohl to emphasize their enormity. By daylight they were the shifting blue of the sea in the Misty Isles; by night, gray but reflecting the torches around us and also seeming to smoulder with interior fires. (*There were fires in Hora, banked since the death of our parents, which even I, her cousin, could not divine . . . yearnings, laughters, sorrows.*) I knew that she used her eyes to feign whatever feeling suited the situation, except alone with me, and then they were often merry, sometimes sad, sometimes indecipherable. Do not misunderstand. We were never lovers, Hora and I. From the time of the loss about which we never spoke—you see, our family had owned a villa and slaves in the Delta of Lower Egypt—Hora had been like a sister to me. (A sister for whom one procures a lover instead of a husband. But Hora and I agreed that marriage was a curse from the gods. "Look at Zeus and Here.")

"It's *sole* survivors," she said. Her eyes were ovals of desperation.

"They can't attack you here, my sweet."

Gratitude.

"And you will want to stay until you can catch another ship. And of course you will need a gown. Your disarray is charming, but our nights are sometimes chill." He snapped his fingers; a young Libyan, black

16

as an onyx blade, appeared at his side. "Horus, you will fetch the lady a gown. A flounced skirt. Blue, I should think. A bodice transparent but not open." To Hora. "Because of the chill. Except for that, I would not diminish your splendors." Horus departed to look for a gown to fit a lady out of the sea.

"It was our intention, my cousin and I, to stay on Pseira. We intended to buy a home. You see, we lived in Memphis, but our parents, our clan, were murdered by cutthroats and thieves, and we wished to forget on these pleasant shores." (In truth there was much to forget, but worse than thieves. . . .)

"Did they rob you as well as kill?"

"Oh, no, Talos. We were spared our fortune at least, though it proved small consolation. Enough however to purchase a house on Pseira and devote ourselves to the pursuits of peace. I am an expert lyrist—I believe you have need for such at festivals?—and my brother is very skillful with the bow. He will enjoy hunting in your forests."

"Not *our* forests. There you are hunted. Now to things of the moment. Our fee for a night's lodging and food is quite reasonable." His face remained smooth; he was not avaricious; he was simply ungenerous, like his trader-countrymen. "More for less" was their ultimate rule, though they rarely stole or lied; they merely out-traded, and the methods they used were as variable as their island: indirectness, evasion, misrepresentation. . . .

"But you don't understand. We lost our belongings aboard the ship. We must wait until our fortune over-

17

takes us. Happily, our gold is following in another ship."

"Oh?" Suspicion narrowed his eyes. "Ships do flounder, as you have seen. A snake in the house is worth two in the garden."

Obviously puzzled, Hora awaited a clarification. In Egypt, snakes had been feared since pre-dynastic times, when arrow heads had been dipped in viper venom.

"The Cretans like a snake in the house," I reminded her. "Bringers of luck, I believe. And fertility, of course. It has to do with their shape, don't you think?"

"A little time, Talos, and we shall have a houseful of snakes."

"I can give you one night." The words, blandly spoken, were unanswerable. "And the gown is free."

"You are too generous." He did not seem to detect her irony; she did not intend detection.

"There are two rooms over the kitchen."

Clashing copper pots, swearing cooks, reek of conch and cuttlefish. Insupportable.

"If you will be so kind as to show us the way." Light as a moth, she brushed his thigh with her hand.

"With pleasure," he smiled, peering at her intently and seeming to like the view. "Your brother shall have this room—"

My room was a cubicle, built I suspect for the least of the cooks. The furnishings were sparse: a raised stone platform without any cushions. "A couch," Talos beamed. A ewer of stale water. "For washing

18

and such." A wooden bench. "For entertaining." A snake-roost shaped like a cylinder. "We are never bothered with flies."

"What about fleas?" At such a time it is best to hold one's tongue. But I lack my cousin's tact. "And where is your vaunted Cretan plumbing?"

"Oh, we reserve that for guests who have not been shipwrecked. You have a chamber pot."

"Bronze, I trust."

"Terra cotta."

The wall which divided our rooms was thin, yellowing parchment of the kind which filled Cretan windows and withstood the sandy blasts from Libya to the south in summer, even across the ridge of Ida, or the Boreal, wintry onslaughts from the north. I could hear Hora's body unfolding onto a cushioned couch; Talos pouring a doubtless delectable wine, or a beer from barley stalks.

"But you must sit beside me. I long for the conversation of a civilized man. The voyage was tedious; the sailors illiterate, to say nothing of disrespectful; the attack a horror beyond description." A touching catch in her voice. "They came at us like a thunderstorm—"

"Poor dear Hora. How you must have suffered. Here, let me bathe your brow. Such golden hair! Is it—?"

"Yes, it is natural. I have no need of dye from the saffron crocus." She did not show offense. She always welcomed a chance to explain that her hair was naturally blonde. "My parents were Achaean, you see.

19

Talos, you presume! We have hardly met, and your hands have begun to explore."

"It is the nature of my race. You must learn our Cretan ways. Desire, explore, possess. You fill my eye, sweet Hora. If I am pleasing to you, well then—"

A sigh which carefully ranged from helplessness to plea. "You would take advantage of a castaway?"

He laughed. "Take advantage? You have much to offer, and your hair is a dazzlement. But then I am hardly a novice in love, and I can promise delights to equal gold." (Always a trader, those Cretans. This for that, skill for gold.) "The choice is yours."

"You must know my answer, you mischievous man."

"How should I know? I lack Egyptian subtlety and you will have to tell me in unmistakable terms. A word or a gesture will do. I only know that there is a dark-eyed Babylonian in an adjacent room. With plumbing. And I never sleep alone."

"If you were to let me linger here for a time. And my cousin too of course."

"Free? *Two rooms occupied?*"

"How else?"

"Hora, dear, you are named for an Achaean goddess, I believe."

"Yes, a goddess of time and seasons."

"But there are connotations to the name."

"How clever of you to spy me out!" Such was Hora's gift. Caught, she would change her approach without so much as a pause. "Yes, I am a courtesan, and I had

20

thought to establish myself at Pseiros. My skills are from Aphrodite. But I need a sponsor."

"We have no courtesans here."

"No courtesans? Such morality! You sound like those guilt-ridden desert folk, the Israelites."

"We have no courtesans because we don't need them. Why pay for a griffin when you can find one in the woods? A night of lodging out of my generous heart. No more."

"Well then, let me enjoy my night alone."

Hardly had he departed than Hora entered my door, bearing a calyx of beer.

"Lordon, did you hear?" She spoke without rancor. She was used to many vicissitudes in her trade. (*"Good and bad are mingled in every life,"* she often said. *"Accept the bad. Exult in the good. And you are ahead of the gods!"* I would have said we had not overtaken them.)

"Everything. Shall I knife him?"

"No."

"Rob him?"

"In his own caravanserai?"

"Perhaps the Libyan lady then. With the plumbing." Other thoughts than robbery pranced in my brain. I have always fancied an older woman. I quaffed the beer in a single gulp.

"No. I expect our host will spend his evening there. I suggest the streets. But the next man you hit, *hit him hard.* I don't want another exile. I like this town. And the men will pay, I promise you that. Just think. I shall introduce prostitution into Pseira. This business of giving free is not to my taste and certainly bad for the trade. After all, I work long hours, and my expenses are great. We have only to find a house, and you shall make friends in the wine-shop and bring me the choicest males. That is to say, the rich and the young. The rich will do. But first to the streets with you."

"Well, I don't mind a little procuring along with my thievery. But I'm overdressed in this Egyptian kilt." With a few vigorous tears I reduced my ancient garment to an abbreviation. "Now I shall look like a fisherman, I expect, and no one shall notice me, and I can skulk and lurk and do my worst."

"Your best." She took my face between her hands and kissed me for luck and smiled. "Did ever a woman have so resourceful a cousin? I wish I could join you. Sometimes I have wished to be a man. But then, being a woman has its own rewards."

I was badly mistaken to steal after such a day, particularly in an alien land, particularly since the young men carry their money in their phallus-pouches, and the old men with money bags—bronze or copper ingots instead of coins—are attended by Lydian slaves. There were also ubiquitous griffins with which to contend. Egyptians like cats. Libyans like monkeys. Cretans like griffins. I can only describe them as huge, four-legged, rainbow-colored birds with long, sloping crests, black beaks as sharp as a fisherman's hook, and a look of eminent satisfaction doubtless learned from their masters. It has often been said that a Cretan will lend you his wife but not his griffin.

Finally I found an old lady asleep in her litter. The bearers must have gone in search of a beer, since crime was hardly known in prosperous Crete. She carried no pouch but she wore a rare pectoral of silver and marguerites about her withered neck, and boldly I started to loosen the leather thongs.

A griffin began to urinate on my foot. I had not seen his approach, but I assured his departure with a forceful kick and resumed my theft.

The motion, however, had waked my victim.

"Young man, are you attempting a rape?" inquired the lady, not without expectation. She resembled a mummy encased in a silver sheath.

"Oh, no, I was only going to rob you."

"Cutpurse!"

The magistrate spoke in a mild, silvery voice. But his meaning was bronze. "You are to leave the city before the sun has set. Thieves are unwelcome to the Griffin Judge." (The Cretans believe that a griffin judges the dead and dispenses punishment or reward.)

I was proud of Hora, who neither flinched nor stammered, but asked a question and stated a truth. "But where can we go? We have no ingots or goods."

"To Phaistos in the south. It faces Egypt, you see, and there are women of your profession to service the sailors." He seemed to belong in the room. Still as stone, he sat on a gypsum chair, and the light from clerestory windows lit the silver bracelets on his arms

23

and kindled the agates set in his belt. Instead of a loin cloth, he wore an ankle-length robe. On the plastered walls, the Griffin Judge, robed like the magistrate, was weighing the deeds of the dead on a monumental scale. Judged, the women were metamorphosing into butterflies, the men into snakes; the evil would keep such shapes; the good would outgrow them whenever they chose—some would choose to linger with those they loved—and join the Goddess in the Isles of the Blest.

"And how shall we find our way to this distant port?" I snapped, looking piratical (or so I hoped) and booming like the surf.

"Distant? The width of the island is thirty-five miles or so at its widest point. Use the sun as your guide. And you can live on the land, which is very rich."

"I am *not* a rustic," said Hora with unaccustomed pique.

"Then learn. Of course you will have to pass through the Country of the Beasts."

"Minotaurs, do you mean? Panisci? Then I would like a sedan chair and a suitable escort of guards."

"Charm them with your golden hair." The quiet young man allowed himself a smile.

"At least we were only exiled," I remarked as we were led from the room by mournful Libyans, slaves from a carefree homeland to the South. "The way they feel about thieves, we might have been sentenced to die."

"But Lordon, we were. No one has ever returned from the Country of the Beasts."

Chapter Two

Lordon

"I think I could be a farmer," I said.

"City boy," Hora chided. "You know how you hate the soil!"

"Not this soil. It's sort of hello before good-bye." . . . . .

The girdling sea an embrace instead of a grasp . . . pine trees to break the occasional storm-wind from the north. Cultivated fields divided by rows of conch shells or multi-colored stones . . . grapevines, laden with clusters of fruit like upturned hives . . . olive trees, silver of leaf, green of fruit, awaiting late summer and beaters with sticks and baskets, the presses, the pressers, the vats and their dragonhead spouts. A summer house, blue as a halcyon, perched as airily in a cluster of vines. . . .

Then, a rise in the land, the cultivation yielding to forestation, with neither a road nor a path to join the work of man to that of the Mother or her irresponsible son.

The Country of the Beasts.

"It's like a cyclopean wall," said Hora, pausing to

nurse a blistered foot. Her feet were unaccustomed to Cretan sandals, but I secretly guessed that she wished to delay our ascent. Walls, unless you know the builders, have to be scaled or breached, and what they conceal is often not what you want.

"It's only pine and cypress, and foliage between. Wild grapevines, bracken, and such."

"Only? They have a look of—judging and passing sentence. Arboreal griffins, a Cretan might say. I don't think we have an invitation."

"Well, we must just invite ourselves."

A row of farmers, grim with scythes and hoes, stood in a human wall (low to be sure, but impossible to scale); behind them, the Libyan guards who had brought us from Pseira watched with the open sympathy which is a mark of their race. Hirelings or slaves, black of skin, exiles from the warm and hospitable south, they understood our plight.

"Well, we can't go back. Even the coastal villagers are alerted to a thief and a whore—"

"Courtesan. Whores take what they can get. Courtesans choose."

"Whatever they called you began with an 'h.'"

"They were speaking my name, I expect."

"I didn't hear any 'a.' Anyway, they might as well have called us Gorgons. One old farmer hit me with his hoe."

"Lordon, Lordon," she smiled. The smile did not deceive me; she meant to allay my fears. "Why are we loitering here when we might be on our way? We've seen worse times. After our parents died—" She did not complete her remark; speak the unspeakable. "I expect we shall see this through." Hora could always summon a smile. She had a thousand likes and a single fear (aside from a Sphinx), and the fear was love, which she shunned like the Ivory Sleep, and I was her devotee.

Thus we entered the Country of the Beasts, lifting a vine, squeezing between two trunks, and the ground rose gradually toward the limestone ridge (snow-clad in winter, snow-clad now in mid-summer where Ida challenged Olympus in majesty) which composed the spine of Crete and halved the island into a temperate north and a semi-tropical south. The sun diminished because of the thickening boughs; brambles prickled our legs; red-capped woodpeckers fluttered from trunk to trunk. At least our captors had allowed me a dagger, its bronze hilt emblazoned with cuttlefish—"you'll need it"—and outfitted Hora in a makeshift tunic, a garment disdained by the women of Crete, which allowed her freedom of movement but enclosed her breasts. "No need to tempt the Beasts."

A griffin flew at us, shrilling, from a clump of shrubs like a Libyan porcupine. Undomesticated, the females have the inclination of Harpies, and they would rather claw you than urinate on your foot. (The males are small and docile, much in the way of a spider male, who is often devoured by his larger mate.) Big as a dog with feathers, she tried to scratch at my eyes, but I brandished my dagger and beat her into retreat. Griffins are cowards, whether pets or loose in the wilds. Other and smaller birds observed us from the branches or from a hill which rose like a turtle from the thickest trees. Owl, oddly awake by day . . . phoenix, preening his daffodil feathers . . . partridge . . . pheasant . . . wood grouse. No fear of hunters in any bird. They seemed to be watching *us*. None of them sang.

"The whole forest is watching," said Hora.

"Ridiculous," I snorted, thinking, however, yes, our arrival is known and observed by every beast (and Beast?).

"Listen!"

At first it was like the drip of a water clock, rapid but scarcely audible even where birds had no song. A friendly sound, unless you must rise with the geese.

But the clocks became manifold; then, the drips were a thump like the hail on a flat stone roof.

"Beasts," said Hora.

"Oh, probably oryxes running from hunters." The oryx was a mountain antelope with black marks and long straight horns; proud, swift, and elusive. I had heard that a few of them lived in the mountains of Crete.

"Lordon, we never lie to each other. It's Beasts, and they're up to no good. Let's make for that hill with the pheasants. It seems to be sunny on top, and at least we can spy out the land and see just what it is that's stalking us."

"Don't you think we should hide?"

"Hide? Where? Everything has its eyes on us."

I gave her my hand; her fingers were moist and limp. Fearless Hora afraid in this fearful land! Tenderness flushed me like the warmth from a sailors' fire, ship drawn ashore for the night. Forests were not for her; she was made for cushions of eiderdown and flaxen gowns and parasols brighter than lazuli butterflies. It hurt. The tenderness hurt. Sometimes I felt such feelings for other folk, and they interfered with my trade. ("Attachments are only for fools," Hora liked to say. I had always agreed with her.)

She patted my beardless cheek (mother with child). Eastern silk was less soft than her supple hand. She stood on her tiptoes and kissed me on the ear. "Little cousin, I'll get you out of this place. See if I don't!"

"Little cousin is grateful, all six feet of him, but let's climb the hill. Something's gaining on us."

"We've been climbing. We don't seem to have made progress. And yet the hill isn't big. Just a hillock, really. Lordon, watch it! You'll fall in that hole!"

"I could swear it wasn't there when I lifted my foot."

"Nonsense. It was overgrown by those Beggar Sticks with burrs."

"Bristly Beggar Sticks, odorous Dog Fennel, Sow Thistles. . . . Are we getting a hint from the hill? No wonder they call this the Country of the Beasts."

"Who's ridiculous now?"

Hills, even conspiratorial, are ultimately climbable, and at last we stood in the sun and looked before us at unbroken trees and behind us at the irrecoverable sea.

Hora sat on a rock. "They might at least have given

us bread and wine. They said we could live on the land, but I've yet to see a stream."

"Here," I said, gathering dewberries from a thorny vine. "They're full and juicy and ought to quench our thirst. Pretend they're beer."

"They're out of season," said practical Hora, straight from Egypt. "Shouldn't be ripe till fall, and it's only mid-summer."

"What do you expect? For a people who hate straight lines and build octangular houses, at least on their islands—well, you can't ask the seasons to behave. It's not like Egypt, where the Nile *always* floods. We'll just have to adapt." I popped a berry into my mouth. "Phew. Tastes like hemlock."

"Adaptation," she smiled. "The first secret of my trade. Yours too, I should think. Phew."

I looked at her in the bright, exposing sun: her face as pink and scrubbed as that of a child, her body lacking adornment of armlet or anklet or even a ring, her hair disarranged and without any fibulae but somehow softer than teased or swirled or trapped by a fillet behind her head. She looked—ripe. No, better than ripe. The mulberry tree had never appeared so bountiful with fruit.

"Hora, if it's any consolation, you aren't a mess."

"Gratifying," she smiled. "If a Beast is going to devour me, at least I shall look my best. I always hoped that when they laid me out for inhumation, they would see to my face and gown. But now I feel undressed. A ring, an anklet, anything would do. . . . Listen. The hoofbeats again."

"You're not going to be inhumed for a good twenty years, and I will dress you in the jewels of a queen, even if I have to steal them." It was a boast and a bluster to hide the hooves, a growing thunder of drums. No longer hesitant, tentative; confident now, gathering, advancing. Thump, thump, thump, they boomed in the undergrowth, circling the hills, building a ring around us, and I thought of a drummer as he drummed an army to war.

"I expect we are going to meet the first of the Beasts."

"May they not be the last," I muttered.

So suddenly did they step from the trees that they seemed at first to be bushes shoved into light. They moved in unison, stood in unbroken unity; gone, the thunder of drums. The silence said, "Wait. Let us observe you. Judge and execute."

"Why, it's only children," laughed Hora. "Dirty at that, and younger than you by far. Satyrs, I should think. And all of them girls."

"Female Panisci. Goat Girls. The kind that stop at the verge of puberty. They look with envy at older girls and their lovers, but never quite understand the meaning of desire. They talk about love as children talk about growing up to become a king or explorer or courtesan. The sailors told me about them on the ship. Some may be forty or fifty years old. Old minds in young bodies."

They climbed the hill, slowly, savoring every step, watching the trapped with the confidence of the trapper, his net and spear in hand. Flanks and cloven

hooves instead of hips and feet. Hair: on their heads
in a riot of dirt; over their naked bodies in matted
clumps. Hard, knowing features with thick red lips
and eyes as yellow as the yolk of an egg. Curving
horns. There was nothing of child about them except
their size and their lamentable lack of breasts. They
reeked of wine and decomposing food and the general
accumulation of those who never bathe. They carried
slings for weapons, and their single garment was a
pouch for stones, attached to a leather belt. They
leaned on each other and laughed and pointed at
Hora and me, and spoke for the first time.

"'Ere, 'ere," said one of the girls. "Always did
fancy a' older man." She sounded as if she had a
briar grape under her tongue. "Right strappin,' I'd
say. And get that goldy 'air. Cor, like 'is mom's."

Hora responded with her medusa look. "It may
interest you to know that I am nobody's mother."

"Grandmom?" sneered the girls.

"Mind your manners, you filthy child."

"I'll get *'er*." said a friend, raising her sling.

"If you will lead us out of this forest, you will find
me strapping indeed," I quickly replied. "And *very*
grateful. I have experience beyond my years. Perhaps
I can teach you to win a man." (Lordon, Lordon,
how you can lie! First you must teach her to grow a
breast.)

"Share and share alike," shrilled a girl whose horns
were overgrown with moss, and whose face was
scarred as if she had been in a fight—or fights. One

of the older girls, I thought. Fifty years to accumulate grievances.

"You are making me sound like a pheasant pie," I said. "But allow me a little time between my engagements, and I will prove a Hercules."

" 'Ercules? Who's 'e? Want action, that's what. Eh, girls?" The Girls responded with a lecherous whinny, though action to them meant—who can say?—knocking me in the head, making a meal of me, or simply boasting to embellish their dream of womanhood and motherhood and ceasing to need a dream. I made a rapid count. Thirty-four . . . five. . . . Well, I would rather be dinner (almost) than lover to such disreputable girls. The smell of them, the look, the sound, was hardly an aphrodisiac.

"Come on down 'ere, sweet 'art."

"Come on up 'ere, girl. Who wants to make love on the side of a 'ill?"

"Airish, are we? Want us to chop it off?"

"Never cut off your ear to spite your face," I replied with, I fear, a notable lack of originality.

"Didn't say 'ear!"

"Lordon," whispered Hora. "I think they mean to kill us. After all, we are useless to them, except as toys to children. And angry children break their toys. Look at the hate in their eyes."

"I imagine they envy you."

"But why? They called me your mother!"

"Because of their envy. Your age, your beauty, your poise. You've grown up. They can't. If I can just pacify them with some sweet talk. . . ."

"All thirty-six?" Like me, she was good at quick calculations. "Look at the blood on the fur of the girl with crooked horns. Not her own, I expect."

"But they're only children," I said. "Perhaps they mean to scare us and nothing more." Perhaps I could reassure Hora if not myself.

"Was anyone ever so cruel as a child who has not been trained? Have you ever watched a baby tear the wings off a dragonfly? To them, we're dragonflies."

"I thought you said toys."

"Either is breakable."

"Less talk and more action, man. Throw us the old cow and follow 'er down."

I clutched Hora's hand. "We'll fight," I said.

"Two against thirty-six. They have slings."

"I have a dagger."

A sudden whirring startled the air, like the sound of a bee surprised into flight. Hora shoved me onto the ground and the stone flew over my head. Quickly I climbed to my feet; rather, I started to climb. The hill began to shake. Beggar Sticks stabbed me as I fell on my knees, momentarily befuddled, and tried to think how a strappin' warrior could save 'is mom. Another bumblebee whirr. Hora flung her body in front of me and took the stone in her hair. Whether it probed to her scalp, I could not say. Anger welled like Lambkill within my throat. Impotent anger; cruel and careless children.

The Girls reached the top of the hill, and a childish face, level with mine, reminded me of another place,

35

a person . . . yes, the Harpy aboard the ship. ("*The lady is dead!*")

The Girls engulfed me with a tangle of limbs. I hardly had time to notice their stench, I was so preoccupied with protecting my face from their blows. Ugh. A kick in the shin. Ugh. The rake of fingernails down my naked back. It seemed that they were adept at breaking toys.

Suddenly there was a stillness like—how shall I say?—the time before the Harpies attacked our ship: a clear blue sky, a pause, and a black inundation. This was just such a time. The ships that the Girls meant to sink were Hora and me.

"Goin' to give me a kiss, sweet'art?"

I kissed her juicily, valiantly on the mouth. She wiped her lips and scowled. "*That* was a kiss? 'Aven't been missin' a thing." The voice was single but it spoke for the group.

"If you would ask politely—"

"All right then, Girls. 'Ensbane, you take the left arm, I'll take the right. Bindweed and Fennel, the legs. If we all pull together—"

"What about the 'ead?"

"Best for last. Pull!"

"CRY SILVER BELLS!"

A woman stood at the foot of the hill. I did not have time to distinguish her form or her face. I saw a blur of green, but somehow I knew that the green was not of our foes, the forest, the shuddering hill.

"Silver Bells?" I asked.

"Silver Bells!" she repeated, her voice resounding

37

like a conch shell from hill to trees and echoing through the piney fastnesses. "For the sake of the Goddess!"

The Goat Girls were gone. . . . Green stood above us, beside her a man with silver bells on his horns. He knelt to my cousin; Green knelt to me.

He was my first friend. . . . She was my first love.

Then I tumbled into the fountain of sleep.

Chapter Three

Zoe

"Moschus, will you heave your smelly carcass onto your side of the couch? I feel downright mummified. Four legs, two arms, and an untrimmed mane are a bit much. Also, you have a paunch."

"Used not to object," he snorted. "Said I had the horsiest hug in the forest." (Understand that a Centaur hugs with his arms and not his forelegs. It is widely and incorrectly assumed that he does not have any arms.) "Got all of you in one grab." He lay petulantly on his back, appendages thrust in the air like a minor forest.

"That was three hundred years ago. And you didn't have a paunch."

"Four hundred."

"You could never add," I snapped. "At any rate, I am not a sapling, and you, my dear, are scarcely a colt." Poor, awkward Moschus. No one expects a Centaur to be at his best in bed. But Moschus was not at his best in the forest. Usually drunk on pomegranate wine, he wobbled instead of cantered among the trees or leaned against a trunk to daydream or snooze. Still, one forgives his friends their little foibles (mine is a disinclination to sleep without a mare. I sometimes find myself with mannerless males. I have even made do with a Faun).

"Time to get up anyway," he said. "Got to see to my pigs." He rolled to the floor but landed on his back, and I had to help him climb to his hooves and guide him down the circular stairway in my tree. Steps had been cut in the wood, but meant for a Dryad's feet and not a Centaur's hooves. The light of the morning shone through windows cut like stars in the living bark. (I had hurt my father tree, but not interfered with his sap. I think he understood. At least I had asked permission before I cut, and trees, like Dryads, want to look their best.)

"And my patients are starting to rouse." A medley of barks, neighs, and screeches greeted my ears and called me to my rounds. "Yes, the day has begun."

"Tonight, old girl?" he whinnied. He smelled of rancid wine and anyone else would have wanted to trim his mane. Still, he had been my friend since the end of the Golden Age—we had played together when Saturn sat on his throne—and friends are to be loved instead of changed.

"I've plans," I lied. Even with Moschus there were times to lie. I must think of my human prisoners.

"Time for a morning libation." He smacked his lips and blinked his bloodshot eyes.

40

"Work to do."

He departed to look for one of the many flasks he had hidden in the woods. To Moschus, a tree stump or cave meant a hiding place, and the object to hide was a skin of wine or beer.

"Aunt Zoe!"

The younger folk call me "Aunt." Actually, some of them *are* my nieces and nephews. My sisters, who live in another part of the forest, are fertile in contrast to childless me, and their mates have been Fauns, Centaurs, and Minotaurs. . . . Dryads, you see, are never male. The daughters are Dryads like their mothers, but the sons take after their fathers. It is often such with the folk of the Country. "Friendly differences": thus had the Goddess decreed when she set the island of Crete on the back of a giant bull.

The speaker, however, was neither a nephew nor niece.

"Yes, Dear?"

Phlebas was none too bright, and, being a male Paniscus, he would never become a man. His body was that of a boy (plump). His mind was that of a child (dense). But his heart was as big as a coconut.

"*Strangers.*" He emphasized the word. He might have said "Sphinxes" or "Harpies." A hopeless romantic, he liked to invent disasters or wonderments, or whisper an escapade and pretend himself a part.

"Where?" Better to humor him. Sometimes he told the truth in spite of himself, since escapades in the forest were as multitudinous as the cones on a fertile pine.

"A man and a woman. Hair's *gold*." His pointed ears gave a quiver of disbelief.

Another one of his tales? Nobody, not even the Lady before she died, had golden hair in the Country of the Beasts. Green for Dryads like me; blue for the Naiads; brown for Panisci and Satyrs; red for Silver Bells, the Minotaur, and his nephew, little Eunostos; black for Harpies who glare at us from the sky.

"Hurry up, Phlebas. Say what you have to say. I must see to my patients."

He never liked to be hurried, but he is somewhat in awe of me. I have given him rich material for his tales about escapades.

"Climbing Bumpers, the hill. And my female cousins hot on their trail."

Bumpers was not a reliable hill—old, crotchety, he hates to be climbed—and Phlebas' female cousins were much the most disreputable inhabitants of the Country, foul-mouthed, scroungy, not above killing animals just for the sport. They had even connived with Humans on occasion and, I suspect, accepted bribes from the Cretans to help them capture Beasts for the Games in Knossos and Phaistos. If there were truly strangers on the hill, they needed immediate help.

"You're sure? You're not just making this up?"

"Cross my heart." He rolled from hoof to hoof and his fat flanks resembled hams with fur.

"Show me to them."

When I was a girl, nobody—Human, I mean—invaded our Country without being eaten by wolves. Well, the wolves had vanished into the higher hills, and now we have a strumpet with yellow hair. I always say, "If you've got it to give, give it free," but she had the nerve to *charge*, or so she had confessed when I helped her to my trees, and the youngster, her cousin, had worked as a pimp and thief! But the Lady—Alyssum, I mean—would never have left them to the murderous girls. Like her, I must summon Silver Bells, and of course he had rapidly put the girls to flight and helped me carry the victims to my Asklepion (most of those wretched children love the man. He had only to shoo them like carrion flies).

Now, the boy was appraising me from his couch. His open eyes, kingfisher blue, did not hold thoughts of theft. He was much too comely, however, like Silver Bells. A girl must beware of such men. And all of that yellow hair. . . . I tried to pretend it to gray, but it winked at me in the window light. I felt—maternal.

"You saved our lives," he said. His couch was a pallet of soft ibex skins. Modest niceties punctuated the room: a cypress chest with flying fish on its lid, painted with ochre and umber. A niche in the wall for the Goddess, gentle in terra cotta. Cat-tails, sleek in a rock crystal urn. It was my finest room, in a tree with foliage like a Pharaoh's hood. But then, he had needed care. . . .

"Nonsense. Silver Bells saved you."

"But it was you who called him."

"I couldn't let you be roughed by those rowdy girls, now, could I?"

"Is Hora all right?"

"Fine. Sleeping, I think. (Think? Knew. Pampered women like Hora sleep or ply, and weaving, sweeping, healing they leave to their slaves.)

"I suspect they were going to tear us limb from limb."

"I doubt it." No need to alarm him. The problem was what to do with him and his whorish cousin. Return them to the coast and their human friends? We love our Country and do not want invaders or even visitors.

"Well, they certainly gave me a wrench. My arms feel unhinged."

"Here. Rub some hog grease into the sorest places."

"That's all right. The ache is starting to go."

"I like you," he added. "You look like a mother, but not the elderly kind. A woman whose husband would never want to stray."

"Nonsense. You don't even know me. Besides, I haven't a husband." Thief talk, I thought. Lower my guard with a compliment. Steal my urn or my chest. The next thing I know, he will compliment my looks, though my three hundred years—I have rounded the number, a woman's privilege—have left me with ample hips, a streak of gray in my moss-green hair, and wrinkles under my eyes—after an orgy, at least. (Not that I haven't my charms. . . .)

"Of course I know you! I get to know people in my trade. You make me think of a fig tree laden with figs. Hora is more the mulberry type. You're for bed and babies. Hora is just for bed. Both are nice. I'm a thief, by the way."

"I guessed. I get to know people too. It shows in your build and eyes."

"Do I look *depraved?*" He gave a piratical wink and seemed to hope for a "Yes."

"No. Just mischievous."

"Oh, I shall have to practice, I guess. Well, I won't rob *you.* Your house is beautiful. Houses, I should say. What do you call your village?"

"An Asklepion. After Asklepius, god of healing. You see, I have my particular tree, as Dryads do. But I come and go as I please, so long as I always return, and the empty trees around me—well, I put them to use. I made them into houses for the sick. And then there's my Incubation Hall under the ground. Those I can't diagnose I put in a row of beds. Asklepius comes to them in a dream and tells them the cause of their pain, or even effects a cure."

"Lucky for Hora and me."

"Hora you say? The name won't do. Silver Bells has suggested 'Marguerite.' He says she reminds him of the marguerite daisy." (*I* would have said an Aphrodite Fly-Trap.) "Its yellow disk, don't you see. I guess he has flowers on his mind. Losing

45

Alyssum, I mean, and less than a year ago. And what about a name for *you?*"

"Well, certainly not a flower, unless it were Hades-in-a-Bush. Do I have to have a new name?"

"One that suits. Eunostos used to be Perdix, but Alyssum said that Perdix suited a partridge, so she called him Silver Bells. He was always rescuing folk, and whenever he did, his bells would shake and tinkle to frighten the griffin, the Human, whatever the kind of threat. The name was exactly right for him."

"How about 'Oryx'? I always liked the animal. Swift and strong like a thief. Able to hide, if he must."

"None of them hereabouts. Wolves devoured them before I was born. But the name has a pleasant ring. All right, Oryx. You can help me with my rounds."

"Are you a proprietess as well as a healer?" he asked. "After all, there are various ways of healing. Somebody may just be lonesome. Hora—that is, Marguerite—is a courtesan."

"I know."

"She has her own particular medicine."

"I have no doubt."

"She could pay you back for all of your help. Work for our keep, as it were. And I might visit a neighbor and—" I saw an eager twitch in his fingertips.

"I don't want to be paid," I said. "and I'm not a proprietess. I'm a healer. The sick come to me and

46

I set their broken limbs or rout their demons of fever. That's not to say I haven't a taste for fun." I thought of my Nubian lover in his tiger skin. The Babylonian with his medical (and other) skills. The Centaurs, the Satyrs. . . . well, my gifts have been bountiful. Gifts, I repeat. I have *never* charged.

The trees in my Asklepion were joined by swaying walkways of skin and rope, and every tree held a different patient, a different demon of pain. He followed me gingerly over the first walkway and into a tree where a Bear of Artemis, a little girl with a nub for a tail and fur instead of a gown, was coughing violently on her couch. She wore a circlet of violets in her hair. It was my children's tree. Bullfrogs carved from pomegranate rinds adorned the chest. The lamp was a hanging pig of striped clay. A live goose sat on a mossy nest and nursed an egg. When a child was able to leave the couch, I let him search in the chest before I sent him home: he would find a gift . . . a scarab, a slingshot, a tail-ring.

"All right, Melissa. Let's see to that cough."

"May I help?"

"If you like. Here. Make friends with Melissa and give her this rocket to nibble." I waited for her to bite his hand. The purple flower, though decorative, tastes like a jimson weed, and making friends would not be an easy task. Melissa hated vegetables, strangers, sickness, big, brotherly-looking boys—all in all, her disposition was not of the best in my tree. But I was testing Oryx. Was he only good as a thief?

He took the rocket, wrinkled his nose, and sat on the pallet beside the child.

"It'll help your cough," he said.

She bit his hand.

With hardly a wince he withdrew the hand and began to eat the rocket.

"Very well. I'll eat it myself." Chomp. "Uhmmmmmm. Delicious." Chomp.

She coughed violently and snatched the rocket out of his hand. The cough subsided with each succeeding bite.

"Feel any better?" another mistake. She glared at him and showed her teeth. Bears of Artemis, small by nature, resent any debt to larger folk. They feel that they ought to do everything for themselves and prove that their size is not a limitation. Their minds as well as their bodies remain those of children (thus they differ from the Panisci).

Oryx pursued his cure with equanimity. "I had a cousin once who was eaten by a bear. In fact, she was taken home to its cubs and *divided*."

Melissa's eyes grew as wide as daisies spread for the sun. Bear-girls have a horror of altogether bears, who begrudge them their human halves and think of them only as meals.

"*Everything?*"

"Right down to her tail. You see, she was a Bear Girl like you."

She gave him a scornful, "Awwwww. Where's your fur?"

"It's the blood that counts. First cousin once removed was a Bear of Artemis."

(A liar as well as a thief, but I had to commend the lie.)

"Where'd you get that hair? *Yellow*."

"Used to be brown. Sun bleached it, while I was sailoring."

"Got another rocket?"

"Got another cough?"

"Yes."

"Don't hear it."

"It's hidden in my throat." Paw pressed to her mouth, she pretended to stifle a cough.

"I'll ask Zoe."

"Yes, I've got another rocket."

Melissa wolfed it greedily, stem, leaves, and bloom, as if she expected Oryx to want his share.

"Come on," I said. "Other patients to see. And of course you'll want to visit your cousin, of which you seem to have an unusual variety. *If this one ever wakes up*." I did not try to keep the reproach from my voice. I knew that the pampered creature was languishing on her couch, and the chariot-sun had climbed a third of the sky!

"She's used to sleeping late. Works at night," he explained. "Plays the lyre, sings, reads poetry, cossets, dallies. *You* know."

"Yes, I know very well. But we have no truck with

49

whores in the Country of the Beasts. Love isn't meant to be sold."

"My cousin is *not* a whore. It's all a matter of style."

"And how much gold she can get from some poor sailor boy."

"What she gives is better than gold, and she has a special rate for poor sailor boys."

Stubborn brat! Always the last word. Still, he had his charm.

"Besides," he continued, "it was the only way she knew to support us. You see we were orphaned when I was only eleven and she was fourteen. In spite of a late start, she learned every trick in the scroll. The Pharaoh of Egypt recommended her to his nephew." He paused. "That was before I hit his nephew on the head."

"Time for the next patient. Oryx, if you're going to hit anybody on the head—"

"Oh, he deserved it. He didn't want to pay. One expects generosity from a Pharaoh's kin." Then to Melissa. "Good-bye and get well. And watch out for bears."

Melissa followed him with her daisy eyes. Suspicion warred with affection. Those hard-seeming little girls have soft hearts. "Been sailorin', huh, Buddy?"

"Yes. All the way to Achaea and Egypt."

"And didn't get lashed by a sphinx?"

"Too quick for her." Strangely, the banter left his voice. He seemed to forget his game; he seemed to be telling a truth.

"Goin' to spruce my tail?"

"Next time."

"And bring me some fresh violets!"

"A whole basket."

"You made a good start," I said as we left the tree. "Can't baby these girls. Or browbeat them either. Fond of folk, aren't you, Oryx?"

"Yes, I guess I am. Even those I rob. But I don't love *anyone*. Except Marguerite." He paused and cocked his head and looked me quizzically in the eye. "But when I meet a woman like you, a *wordly* woman, I start to wonder if—"

"Ought to have met the Lady." I had known my share of boyish adoration. Flattering, yes. But send me a Minotaur bull like Silver Bells to do a bull's work! (Unfortunately, no one had ever sent him, even before his wedding.)

"Who *is* the Lady? Even a Harpy mentioned her death."

"She was a Naiad, a fountain nymph. Hair as blue as a gentian. Everybody loved her. Harpies, you say? Well, we have no truck with them here. But one of them broke a wing in a gust of wind and crashed in our forest. I wouldn't have her in my Asklepion. But Alyssum nursed her to health. Hadn't a wicked thought, the Lady. But not womanish, if you know what I mean. Said no and meant it to every male in the forest. Then Silver Bells asked, and *he* had to win her with *poems*. Do you know, they were actually wed. Now me, I've had a husband or two in my younger days. But never again. . . ."

"I know what you mean. Marriage is one more shackle on the heart. But where is Silver Bells? I want to thank him."

"You'll see him, and his nephew Eunostos too. You'll get to meet everybody, and then we'll have to decide what to do with you."

"I've already decided to stay in the Country."

"You haven't had an invitation as yet. Or that indolent cousin of yours."

"You mean we're your prisoners?"

"In effect, yes." I tried to look like a gaoler.

"I'm guilty," he grinned. "Keep me in the forest."

"We shall have to consult the Great Centaur. His word is final in matters like this." (He was one of my lovers, of course.)

We visited all of my patients, a blue-haired Naiad who had brushed a Nightshade plant—the deadly kind—and left an ugly welt across her arm; quince and wild purslane, applied in a plaster, quickly removed both the welt and the pain, though more than a brush with that lethal plant would have killed the girl. . . . A full-grown Satyr who had stomped his hoof in a pout and left a painful crack: a splint for him, applied by Oryx with my direction. He was a quick learner. Perhaps it went with his trade. Somehow, though, I thought less often of him as a thief. Perhaps because he had told me how he had come to steal. Perhaps because he was eager to please without being unctuous and soft. Perhaps because there was so much liking in him, whatever he said about love. (And such a wonder of hair! Unexpectedly, I yearned to hold his head against my breast, I who had wanted a child for three hundred years but been denied by the Goddess for reasons I did not know.)

"That cousin of yours is going to have to get up," I pronounced at the end of my rounds. "The sun is directly overhead. Scandalous."

"I'll wake her," he said. "She likes to ease out of sleep."

I led him to her couch in the lowest, scruffiest tree. The couch was a simple pallet of papyrus reeds, and Hora lay tangled intimately with her goatskin coverlet. Like me, she was used to sleeping with a friend.

"Hora," he whispered. "It's Lordon. We're safe from those horrid girls."

I snatched the coverlet off of her (Artemis, what a shape! I could understand, if not forgive, her trade). "Get up, woman," I barked. "I run an Asklepion, not a brothel."

She sighed, and golden ringlets tumbled over her head (and how I envied that hair!).

"And who are *you*?" she inquired with a decorous smile, but as if it were she who owned the place, and I the visitor.

"The owner, that's who."

"And I am Silver Bells." In spite of his bells, I had failed to hear his approach. With him was his nephew, little Eunostos. They were the last of their race, the magnificent Minotaurs. Silver Bells' sister, Eunostos' mother, I mean, had strayed from the Country and caught a hunter's spear. Her grief-stricken husband had died from the Ivory Sleep. Eunostos was only eight, and his uncle treated him like a small brother, taught him to hunt and garden and made him a bow and quiver and a peaked, moss-green cap with a feather plucked from a woodpecker's tail. A Minotaur is a versatile Beast, and he does not think it would be beneath him to garden or toil in a work-shop as well as to hunt and fight; an affectionate Beast, who will hug his nephew as soon as his niece. He is also a natural poet and an omnivorous reader of scrolls. Silver Bells' one real fault was a total inability to cook. I had to bring him pheasant or partridge pies, pokeweed salads and possets flavored with thyme, to insure that Eunostos would have a proper diet. Left to themselves, they would have subsisted on honey cakes.

I turned to greet them, but they were looking at *her*.

"Silver Bells! Now I remember. It was you who saved us."

"You didn't take much saving. The girls are cowards with one who knows their ways." It is hard to describe the speech of a Minotaur. It is dreamlike and musical as befits a poet, and yet it is of the earth as well as the sky.

"You have a distinguished air about you, Sir." (It was she who had the air. Airs, I should say.) "A court-liness all too rare in these barbarous times. May I ask, uh, the name of your race? I notice several becoming appurtenances."

A Minotaur's horns are not like those of a goat.

They resemble the antlers of a stag, and he, of course, wore tiny silver bells with golden clappers. Whenever he moved, he resembled singing birds. His face was shaved—he shaved every day with a bronze razor dipped in a thermal pool—and his hair, though long, was caught behind his head with a copper ring, displaying his pointed ears. Red as a woodpecker's crest, it suited his ruddy skin. In other locations, hair abounded but always under control. Chest. Legs. Loins (and fortunate too, since he wore no loin cloth. Not that a Beast would notice such a lack, but city-bred courtesans never miss a trick.) And of course the tail, long, slender, tufted with gossamer down. Minotaurs pride themselves on their versatile tails. They use them to grasp objects, to flick insects, to display for the females who catch their eyes. Part of their courtship lies in the nimbleness of their tails. (But Silver Bells seemed to have lost his vanity when Alyssum had told him. "You may stop showing off, my dear. It isn't your tail I love.")

"I *particularly* like your tail," concluded Marguerite.

She's got him, I thought. *If she knows how to cook.*

Then I remembered how lately his wife had died, when those arena people had caught her in their net (she had fought, and failed, and willed herself to die, rather than act in their games). No, I decided, *she* wants *him,* and she won't even make him pay! To Silver Bells, she is only a guest from the coast.

"Marguerite," said a small, manly voice. "My uncle and I have brought you some wine." Adoration rounded Eunostos' eyes. He straightened his cap and stood to his fullest height. Men! Even at eight, you can catch them with golden hair.

The airs disappeared from Marguerite's manner and speech. She received the wine as if it had come from Egypt. "Young man, you remind me of my cousin. You know how to treat a lady." (Indeed!)

"My uncle says that ladies reflect the Goddess, and one is always to show them manners."

"Not all of them," I muttered, but nobody seemed to hear.

"Your uncle is a rare gentleman. Come, Eunostos, and sit beside me."

Lightly she bent and kissed his head. I will have to say that it seemed a natural move. She was cleverer than I had thought. *Woo the child, win the man.*

She must, however, work with a Siren's speed.

The Great Centaur had yet to decide her fate.

Chapter Four

Zoe

I would have to give an orgy.

The Great Centaur, Chiron, had not yet delivered judgment on Oryx and Marguerite (not that I cared about *her*, but I liked the boy, and I wanted a chance to teach him not to steal). Chiron was generally just in his pompous way, but, since he was one of my lovers, I thought that I knew how to bend his justice to the aid of my guests. He was much too timid, in spite of his regal airs, to execute them, but much too suspicious—and not without reason—of Humans to let them remain in the Country of the Beasts. However, if he returned them to the coast and their own people, they might reveal our riches—and weaknesses—and invite invasion. We liked to preserve our reputation for ferocity and inviolability. He would doubtless set them adrift in a cockleshell of a boat, and the careless Tritons would drive them from Crete. Thus, they would either drown or end at a Siren's feast.

That is to say, unless I changed his mind.

The Great Centaur liked formality and loved an au-

dience. On such an occasion, I could not invite him
to a tete-a-tete in my tree. I must ply him with food
and drink in the company of selected guests to ap-
plaud his aphorisms, admire his majesty. I must
flatter, cajole, manipulate, and only then present my
dessert and plead for my visitors.

In the Country, everyone works for himself, and
I had neither slaves nor servants to help me prepare
for the evening (or attend to the sick in my trees).
But Marguerite and Oryx, knowing their fate to be at
stake, and Oryx, out of sheer generosity, proved
adaptable helpers. To my astonishment, Marguerite
was extremely knowledgeable about the care of the
sick, the mending of bones, the preparation of herbs;
she attended my patients while I prepared the food;
and Oryx, carrying a bow as well as a fishing net,
ventured into the forest after game for the evening
(we never kill animals—except for aging pigs to get
their skins—but we do eat birds and fish). Others
helped too: Melissa left her sick bed to gather violets
in the woods, and Phlebas scattered tables and wooden
benches among my trees.

Preparations completed, Marguerite, Oryx, and I,
tired but exhilarated by the challenge ahead of us,
lounged in the grass beside my hyacinth pool and
awaited our guests. (I had ordered Phlebas to bathe
and Melissa to rest and eat another rocket.) I tried to
prepare the cousins for their meeting with Chiron.

"Above all, if he quotes an aphorism, pretend you
think it's his own. *Never* confess that you've heard it
before, though of course you will have several hun-

dred times. He has a way of appropriating and claiming to be the author. He tries to act both learned and wise, but truthfully he's—"

"Dumb," said Oryx.

"Let's put it more tactfully. Slow. A Great Centaur has always ruled the Country, but Chiron sort of toppled into his position when his father and older brothers were killed by wolves. He's forgotten the circumstances, though. He thinks he was born to rule. As long as you make him feel strong, knowledgeable, handsome—a great lover—you're all right. Otherwise—well, I made him angry once when I temporarily broke off my dalliance with his cousin, Moschus, and he punished me by imposing chastity for a month! Can you imagine? You would have taken me for a pinched little virgin. I lost my color as well as my appetite, and I grew my first gray hairs. Of course, at the end of the time, he compensated in generous measure. And then I reconciled with Moschus."

"I wonder," said Marguerite. "Can I help? I do have my trade." She appeared both earnest and touching; with me, she had dropped her airs and, though garbed in a torn and colorless tunic, her only garment, she somehow managed to look like a gold-haired Alyssum. But such a crude suggestion!

"Sell your favors?" I cried. "*Charge* the Great Centaur?"

"Oh, no, you misunderstand!"

"I suppose you will ask for copper ingots. Or gewgaws perhaps?"

"I intended to *give*. At the moment, it's all I have, you see."

Chastened, I said, "I'm sorry, my dear, but he has no truck with Humans. I have already chosen the proper dessert." (Really, how could there be any question?)

We heard a silvery tremble of bells at the gate (if I were more of a poet and less of a realist, I would claim a similar tremble in my heart. More accurately, there was a thump.)

Silver Bells was always punctual. To him, Cockroost time did not mean Owlhoot time. He arrived in a splendor of mane and hooves and tail, but his good-humored kiss could not conceal his concern for the fate of my guests.

"Zoe," he said. "Things will go well, I promise. You arrange such congenial orgies." He squeezed my hand in a brotherly fashion.

"Thank you, my dear. And I see you've brought Eunostos." I gave my goddess-child a kiss on his pointed ear. "I've made some plans for the young. Eunostos and Melissa"—she had left her couch—"and Phlebas"—fresh from a bath, he looked of an age to draw a bow and even read a scroll, but his mind had lingered at six. "My Incubation Hall is empty of patients now. I've arranged exciting games—knucklebones, toss-the-toad, what-have-you. And yes, there are honey cakes. Then you can roast the meat for the older folk. Melissa will be in charge. (Eunostos could not roast a woodpecker, much less a pheasant. Like his uncle, he tended to ruminate and burn the meat.)

"Honey cakes! I think I'll join Eunostos," grinned Silver Bells. (Zeus, what a Beast! Little did he know that I secretly quivered whenever he smiled at me.)

"You'll stay right here. You must help me to soften Chiron. Get him to like our visitors. Don't you want them to stay?"

"Don't you want us to stay?" said a honeyed voice. It was Marguerite. She had disappeared from the group when Silver Bells knocked at the gate and reappeared in a tunic which I had loaned to her for the evening. Since I am considerably more voluptuous, I had never meant her to look her best (I had meant her to look like a sack). But slyly she had contrived to find the time in which to alter the garment until it clung to her like a tunic to Artemis. It revealed both arms and legs and one of her ivory shoulders, and what I saw was what men like. She had failed to fillet her hair. Carelessness? Calculation! It tumbled over her shoulders like a rain of crocuses.

Silver Bells smiled at her with suitable admiration but not with desire. Alyssum was rarely out of his thoughts. "I want you to stay very much," he said. "You've won Eunostos' heart; you know. He's brought you a gift. And one for our hostess too."

Eunostos, wearing a bulla or hollow, frog-shaped amulet around his neck, and little more—that is to say, like his uncle, whose more was an agate ring to restrain his hair—presented his gifts to Marguerite and me with one simultaneous motion (his uncle had taught him impeccable manners): for me, a Centaur carved from cedar wood, for Marguerite, a wreath of

61

the daisies which had inspired her name, and hidden among them, a delicate pendant, a silver butterfly with filigree wings.

"I thought of Zoe's gift by myself," Eunostos said, "but Uncle Silver Bells thought of the pendant for Marguerite. He said he had named her for Marguerite Daisies, but she might not like them. They might be too simple for a city girl."

"Too simple?" she cried. "I love them. More than blue lotuses from the Pharaoh's pool!" (I thought I saw a tear on her cheek.) She hugged Eunostos against her breast, and just for a selfish moment I wished the Great Centaur to put her adrift in a boat and a Siren to carve her for lunch! (I never claimed that all of my thoughts were kind—not about courtesans with an eye for Silver Bells.)

"I'm here," said Oryx, joining Marguerite. He wore a garland of columbine. His hair, like that of his cousin, rioted gold. He looked like a prince of the woods. Except for the color, he looked like one of us (I forgave his pointless ears).

"We've *been* here," said Melissa and Phlebas in unison, clearly wanting attention. Her tail was immaculate, her violets fresh; and Phlebas smelled of clover instead of goat. I heard him muttering to himself, "An *orgy*. Wait till I tell my friends!"

Someone . . . something . . . it seemed . . . had come with Silver Bells. A butterfly, saffron and delicate as a snowflake with wings, hovered above his head. There are those who claim that she is the soul of the Lady, returned from the land of the Shades to

62

rejoin her husband; or at least that Silver Bells thinks her to be his wife. Whatever the truth, he turned and lifted his head and looked at the butterfly, and I could swear that she was sending him thoughts. . . .

Nectar and daffodils, sunlight and dragonflies. . . . *Do not grieve for me, love, for wings have made us one* . . . Foolish Zoe! Such thoughts should be left to poets. She was probably a simple butterfly, after my flowers.

We entered my Asklepion, which I had walled with tall and bristling timbers in the time of the wolves. A low, mossy hill (not ill-tempered like Bumpers) rises along my trees, and tonight she held the tables for my feast. I had heaped them with the rarest delicacies of the forest—dog-berries mixed with horse-gentians; spitted pheasants ready for roasting; wines of every description, from grape to gooseberry, and of course beer, *horse-sugar* beer, the favorite of Centaurs and especially Chiron, in great bulging pigskins. A Centaur could lift a skin, remove a cork from the snout, and aim a luscious stream unerringly toward his mouth. For light, I had hung the trees with lanterns (a gift from the East, brought to me by a younger Moschus when he sought my hand in marriage). They were made of an Eastern substance known as *paper,* a sort of thinner papyrus, which revealed the candles and yet enclosed their light, and they were shaped like the sunbird of the East: small, but yellowly bright with feathers and crest. In effect, I had illumined the night with paper birds of day, since Chiron professes

a keen aesthetic sense and claims to appreciate inno-
vation in every area (I can only vouch for one).

He arrived in a cavalry-burst of clattering hooves
and jangling bells, replete with a royal escort and his
cousin and drinking companion, Moschus. Of course
he had a wife; six, I believe; but when the Great
Centaur attended an orgy, he left his wives in the
stall. We pride ourselves on equality between the
sexes in the Country, but the Centaurs acquired
some customs, along with artifacts, on their wander-
ings through the East.

"And how is my esteemed friend Zoe," he asked,
courteous, even affable, but not forgetting his dignity,
his royal station and attendant power, and peering
over my shoulder at the beer and the meat. He wore a
green blanket of spider-silk, edged with murex-
purple, across his back. His crown of jade, much too
broad for his narrow head, was a gift from an Eastern
king.

"In excellent spirits, my Lord, and much improved
by your coming." (He dotes on formality when others
are watching. Moschus was watching and restraining
a neigh; I thought him a trifle unsteady on his hooves.
Perhaps he had nipped before he left his stall or managed a snort en route from one of his tree stumps or
caves.)

Chiron clapped his hands and his escort of four
brawny males, brandishing wooden spears above their
heads and wearing leather jerkins around their shoulders, vanished noisily into the woods. Their manes
were turbulent; their pectorals glittered garishly even

in lantern light and jangled instead of sang. The usual Centaur prides himself on his dress, but these were the toughs of the wood, the so-called Whinnies, chosen no doubt because they liked to fight.

"And these are my—p-prisoners," I stumbled introducing Oryx and Marguerite. I would have liked to call them my guests, but Chiron could only see them as interlopers. At this point, I did not want to endanger their case.

"Not bad for Humans," he said, as he straightened his crown. "Boy's a swift runner, that's for sure. Woman must be good for a dozen or so colts—uh, what is the Human word?—babies."

Moschus mumbled under his breath, "Don't you mind, Marguerite. He describes everybody that way. You're good for much more than colt-bearing. Anybody can see that."

I stooped and bathed Chiron's hooves with a cloth dipped in myrrh and then I led him into the Asklepion. He observed Eunostos, Melissa, and Phlebas and said, "I'm sure you youngsters have plans of your own. Games or something. You're dismissed."

"I've composed a poem in honor of your visit, my lord," Eunostos said.

"Oh, a panagyric perhaps? On with it then."

> The moose
> Is loose.

"Yes, yes, finish the poem, my boy."

"I *have* finished, your honor. But I have another."

"*One* was enough."

Beware
The bear.

"Dismissed!"

Eunostos, bowing with childish dignity, led his friends into the Incubation Hall. ("I want to stay and watch," said Melissa. "Hush," said Eunostos, polite but firm.)

"Aunt Zoe," he called to me over his shoulder. "Give a shout when you want us to roast the meat."

"Burn it, you mean," snorted Moschus, who supped from time to time—all of the time, I should say—with his forest friends and had suffered a meal prepared by Eunostos and Silver Bells.

Silver Bells looked displeased at such an abrupt dismissal of the children, but what can you say to a king?

Leave it to him to find the words. "My Lord, they would have entertained us with their games."

"Poems, more likely."

I settled the Great Centaur against a tree, a sapling with foliage like a Dryad's hair, and he rubbed his back and sighed and promptly announced.

"I should like a flagon of beer. And a pheasant. Skip the salad. And bring me a flagon of beer."

"You've already ordered a flagon," reminded Moschus. Drink had loosened his tongue.

I gave him a warning look.

"And how is my old friend Silver Bells?" asked Chiron. Even the Great Centaur did not condescend

66

to *him*. They sometimes engaged in a wrestling match or a game of draughts, and Silver Bells wisely allowed the King to win; however, in other ways he refused to play the courtier and remained unalterably a Minotaur (and the best of his race since the Golden Age). Chiron in fact had performed the wedding rites for Silver Bells and Alyssum (after innumerable attempts to win her for his own seventh wife).

I looked at Silver Bells in the light of the sunbird lanterns, the last adult Minotaur, and my heart, itself a bird, flew out to him in his grief and loneliness (and also because, quite frankly, I would like to get that Beast into my couch). His mane was caught with a malachite ring; hair rippled fierily down his chest and loins; modesty kept him from guessing his own magnificence. True, he had his vanities—he was proud of his poems—but they made him all the more Beastly and lovable.

He smiled at me and must have guessed my apprehensions for Oryx and Marguerite.

"Zoe, will you honor us with a song?"

"Why, I don't know if I can—what do you think, Chiron?" Actually, I have a more than passable voice and an extensive repertoire, but I did not know if the Great Centaur wanted a song with his beer. (I knew what he wanted *after* his beer.)

"Oh, very well," he sighed, handing an empty gourd to Oryx to refill.

"A drinking song, my Lord?"

"I shall leave it to your discretion. But make it brief." His look was aphoristic.

67

I sang a drinking song of his own composition (for once he had failed to steal, a mistake at best). I sang less to please his ear than arouse his appetite:

> See what the Beasts in the back room will have
> And bring them more of the same:
> Horse-sugar beer
> And me, my dear,
> And mine is the liveliest game.

Chiron revealed a flicker of interest at the word "game" and then stared aphoristically into his beer.

I pranced into a whirling dance (I am told that in spite of my geographical splendors, I dance like a temple maiden); I flung my arms as if to bestow a bounty (or promise a bounty to conclude the evening); my hair was a living garland aswirl above my head, and the lantern light concealed the streaks of gray.

"More, Zoe, more!" shouted Oryx.

(Appreciative boy!)

I awaited acclamation from Moschus, but the beer had gone to his head and he leaned with beatific oblivion against a tree.

"Everybody now!" I cried.

> See what the Beasts in the back room will have
> And bring them more of the same. . . .

"You sang that nicely, Zoe. Now shall we wax philosophic?" asked Chiron. "It's rather expected at orgies." A perfect chance to plead for my prisoner-guests.

"I'm no philosopher," I began.

"No, you're not."

"*But* it seems to me that the Goddess didn't create this island and set it aback a bull and, for all we know, the world, and set it aback a turtle, without a pattern.".

"An excellent discourse," said Chiron. "Shall we hear from the Guest of Honor?" Silence. "The Great Centaur?"

"Opposites," I repeated. "Everywhere. Obvious ones like night and day, life and death, good and evil. Geographical ones like earth and water. Living ones, like a Sphinx and a Minotaur."

"You've made your point, my dear."

"My point is that Humans, like Beasts, are sometimes good, sometimes bad. My point is that Oryx and Marguerite—"

"*More beer if you please.*" The request was a command. " 'Spirituous beverages increase desire but limit performance,' " he continued. "However, such is not the case with the Great Centaur." He often spoke of himself in the third person.

Oryx had disappeared in the midst of my song. Silver Bells was consoling Marguerite, who looked both small and timorous in so sublime a presence, and not her usual blithe and confident self. (Unlike me, she was not a girl to appreciate Chiron's compliment, "good for colt-bearing.") I must forget the

Muse and fetch the beer, though the second verse was about dessert.

"A whole skin if you please," he added. " 'Tis not the beer but the content/ That makes the Centaur's merriment.' However, the beer helps."

"Hisst!"

It was Oryx, calling to me from behind a tree (Melissa's tree), an elm with a knobby, concealing trunk.

"Do you think he will let us stay?"

"He hasn't made up his mind yet," I said.

"He hasn't much to make up."

"Nevertheless, he requires further diversions."

"Oh," said Oryx sadly. "Zoe, I don't want to go."

"You'll have to if he gives the command."

"But I shall miss you too much!" He looked like a little child who has lost his goat cart or suffered his father's whip.

"And I shall miss you, my dear. But you *must* forget your thievish ways."

"There's something big I wish I could steal."

I cast a rapid eye around my Asklepion and over his person. His loin cloth was not designed for concealment. Still, an admitted thief—!

"What do you mean, Oryx?" I asked, not without trepidation. My lovers had brought me a pharaoh's fortune in hammered silver goblets, ivory elephants from Nubia, incense burners of beaten gold. . . . I cherished them not for their value but for the memories which they evoked of the Golden

Age, and a young girl receiving her first caress, and a young woman receiving a kiss, a caress, and. . . .

"Your heart."

Roguish Oryx! He had lured me into a trap. Little boy was mischievous young man. He seized me in his arms and planted a clumsy but conclusive kiss on my mouth.

Carefully, not wishing to hurt his feelings, I extricated myself from his embrace.

"Oryx"—I omitted the "dear" to prevent a repetition—"I'm a trifle old for you, don't you think?"

"What are a few hundred years between lovers?"

"Oryx, how can you say such a thing? Why, you've only just kissed me!"

"I know, but I have plans."

"LOVERS?"

Zeus save us, it was the Great Centaur, haughty as a pharaoh about to dispose of a slave. Because of my delay, he had come to fetch his beer, and the coming had made him petulant, and the finding of me, his hostess, in Oryx's arms—well, his rage was predictable.

"We shall cast them afloat tomorrow. Humans indeed! All alike, every bloody one of them. 'To err is Human . . . uh . . . uh, etc.' But Zoe, I am shocked at you, a *Beast*."

Chapter Five

Oryx

We sat on three-legged stools in the lowest room of an old and mottled oak. It was usually reserved for terminal cases, sufferers from the White Sleep or the Demon of Fever and Shakes. Fortunately, nobody in the compound suffered such a disease, though the Great Centaur had chosen the room for Marguerite and me with an obvious hope to alarm. Winding sheets lay folded between the pallets, and holy water, blessed with the secret name of the Griffin Judge, rested mournfully in a rock crystal urn. The light from the oval windows was thin and tentative; and Marguerite's roseate face was blanched to the deathly white of a lotus bloom.

"I feel imprisoned," she said.

"You are," I said. "There are Whinnies guarding the door." The only animal-hunters among the Beasts, they wore their leathern jerkins and cracked their ribald jokes. Cocking an ear to catch the latest dirt, I resumed my explanation to Marguerite. "Chiron is taking no chance that we will escape. And one of them told me he's also punishing Zoe. Another sentence of chastity. *Two months.*"

"It's what she deserves, trying to seduce my little cousin. Why, she must have given you the fright of your life. You seem to have shrunk by an inch. And the color has left your cheeks."

"Marguerite, I grabbed her. And I solicited her too. After the grab had failed. I was, you could say, a lecher."

"If you were, she must have enticed you. Poor innocent boy, what do you know about such worldly women?"

"A lot," I said, naming no names. (Was there another kind? Alyssum was dead. Hermes be thanked that little Melissa must always remain a child!) "And she didn't mean to entice me. She was just too delectable to resist."

"She's big in the hips."

"Voluptuous, I would say. A lot of woman, but built to tease and please."

"Zoe exciting? Why, that woman could be my mother. Didn't you notice the gray in her hair?"

"She could be your great-great-great, etc., grandmother, but she somehow manages to improve with age, like an opulent tree, and no, I didn't see any gray, but if I had, it would have just seemed a bit of moss in an oak, and I would have liked it too. Zoe is *one fine woman*, and I won't hear her badmouthed even by my cousin."

"Well, there's no accounting for tastes," shrugged Marguerite. "Now if you're looking for quality—I expect Alyssum had it in generous measure. Otherwise, Silver Bells would never have married her. *He* is the best."

"At least we agree on him. If we weren't going to be deported and drowned or eaten, I had planned to ask him if he would like to adopt us."

"I had thought about something else, but apparently he didn't. He's only thirty, you know." (Indeed? You could never guess the age of a Beast. I suspect that Marguerite had inquired of Zoe.)

"Cousin," I said. "Have we forgotten our vow? No attachments, I mean. We're likely to ruin our trade."

"Not that it matters any more—here come our captors—to lead us to our fate. . . . The same four Whinnies from the night of the orgy."

Leering, ogling, snickering, they led us out of the tree and one of them pinched Marguerite on the cheek and smirked,

"Need a speck o' color in them cheeks, queenie."

I knocked his hand to his side and he gave me such a kick with his hoof that I fell on my back and consciousness fled from me like a light from a wind-blown lamp. It was Silver Bells who lifted me to my feet—I was still befuddled but I heard his bells . . . I thought of a time when I had been a child and both a father and mother had loved and protected me. . . . yes, in the dreadful confrontation. (But memory must be guided, even as speech. I had promised Marguerite.)

He smelled of rue because he often gathered the

aromatic and medicinal plants for Zoe to use in her
potions (before Alyssum had died, he had gathered
thyme). On Silver Bells the herb was a manly scent,
in spite of its feminine name; or rather the scent of a
valiant Beast, whose heart, like the nautilus, holds
several chambers, and one was courage, and one was
tenderness.

"You won't let those bloody Whinnies pinch Marguerite?" I gasped.

"Never again," he said, and I cleared the haze from
my eyes and saw them trotting a cautious distance behind us, and the pincher was nursing a bruise on his
head. Zoe had joined us on the way, and of course
Eunostos, who helped his uncle to lift me from the
ground—strong little chap—and together they stead-
ied my walk. I liked Eunostos, feather atop his hat;
ruddy of skin that would sprout a ruddier hair when
he became a youth; and already blessed with a handsome broad-tipped tail. Suppose he sometimes burned
a pheasant because he liked to dream. Suppose his
poems could use some polish and style. He was only
eight.

"Thank you, Eunostos," I said. "That was quite a
blow I took."

"That Whinny named Horse-Brier took a worse
one from my uncle. I wish you could have seen—"

"So do I, Eunostos." Then to Silver Bells: "I think
I can walk alone, now, with your nephew's help.
Maybe Marguerite needs some consolation."

She did; daylight had not restored her coralline
cheeks. Merry Marguerite, ripe for an escapade,

looked like a walking figure of alabaster, as white and hushed. I could tell from Silver Bell's face that he saw her fear and knew the fearful fate which awaited us, and I could see an anger against the King for his cruel and capricious sentence, and wistful memories of a time when the woods had bellowed with Minotaurs, and no dim-witted, vainglorious Chiron, even a king, could impose such a judgment without a fight. But Chiron employed an army of Whinnies and bribed the Panisci girls to run him errands and spy on peaceful folk. He was not a heartless Beast, he was a cowardly beast; but cowardice borrows from Proteus in its many disguises.

Zoe gave me a sisterly pat on the cheek. Her scent of coriander went to my head. My thoughts were revelers at a festival.

"It was all my fault," I said. "If I hadn't been so lecherous and conniving—"

"It was nobody's fault, except that bigot we call a King."

"But to punish an innocent Dryad—"

"You know, he once asked me to be his second wife —or was it third?—but I declined and I must have hurt his pride. The ones he got apparently haven't sufficed."

"*Two* months this time."

"Oh, I shan't mind too much," she said. "After all, I've weathered a month before. I'll just keep twice as busy. That's the answer. Garden and heal by day, study scrolls at night." (She was trying to ease my concern. She was not an omnivorous reader like Silver

76

Bells. I believe that her favorite scroll was a trashy romance, *Hoofbeats in Babylon*.) "It's you who worry me. You and Marguerite. You don't know these Cretan waters, and you can't just sail down the coast and come ashore or your own people will capture you for the theft you committed on Pseira and give you to the bulls. The magistrate never meant you to reach Phaistos, you understand."

"I know a bit about sailoring. The rest I'll learn."

"You must." She gave my hand a squeeze. Aphrodite forgive me, I thought of a second grab.

At last we came to the ship. An hour-glass could have emptied its sands in the time we took, but the walk passed as quickly as making a theft, except without the fun, and the end of the journey was getting caught in the act.

The ship . . . the boat . . . was old, with one cracked oar, neither seats nor sail, and rainwater in the bottom aswirl with frogs. We found ourselves in a rocky cove where cypresses leaned their heads from over-hanging cliffs like curious ladies at the Bull Games in Knossos or Phaistos (the bull and the Dancer stab each other to death, the one with his horns, the other with short-sword or knife); and sweet-scented thyme grew in clefts and crevices, mocking the scent of the ladies. As for the beach, it looked like a place for thieves to count their loot, but the Great Centaur, in his pique and stupidity, had converted it into a sort of bull-ring, a place of judgment and doom.

Silver Bells waded into the surf, and Zoe joined him. She made no effort to keep the water from wetting her tunic or ruining her sandals of bark.

"You call them, Zoe," he asked. "It's the Tritons we want to hear, and they won't even listen to me. Not since I hoofed their King."

"ALL RIGHT NOW, YOU TRITONS," boomed Zoe. "These are friends of mine and I want you to guide them to a friendly island or find them a merchant ship."

I heard the quietly insolent lapping of wavelets on the beach; I saw the lazuli splash of a kingfisher seeking fish. Otherwise, silence. . . .

"Nobody heard?" asked Marguerite.

"Oh, they heard all right," shrugged Zoe. "It's just that they don't much like anything or anybody on the land. They don't choose to answer."

"Not even Zoe," said Silver Bells, "but they don't dislike her quite so much as the rest of us. They rather fancy her pointed ears."

"Breasts," she whispered to me. "Silver Bells is terribly naive about such things." Then, loudly, "They always want to be paid for everything, but I do have my principles. Besides, for two months, I lack the wherewithal. One little indiscretion and I would follow you in a boat. Not that I wouldn't take the risk if I thought it would help. . . ."

Eunostos pulled the hair-ring from his head and threw it into the bay. Aquamarine, it seemed returning from exile to its home.

"King of the Tritons!" he cried. "Take my gift and protect my friends."

"That was a generous gift," said Marguerite as hair spilled over Eunostos' ears. She knew how he prided himself on his circumspect dress.

"But it won't help, will it?" sighed Eunostos. "I forgot. Aquamarines are like pebbles to a Triton."

"There's really nothing they like on Crete," said his uncle. "But once in awhile you'll find a Triton with heart. He may understand the gesture. I am proud of you, Eunostos."

Marguerite had started to cry. She wore neither kohl and galena to run from her eyes or carmine to streak her face; clear, silent tears diamonded her cheeks; she had learned how to weep in her trade, and not to redden her eyes. A man is only moved by a woman's tears if she does not blubber or spoil her looks. Not that she wept for effect at such a time. But she had forgotten unbecoming tears. I hugged her, and then I turned to Zoe and Silver Bells and said,

"We won't say goodbye. We're going to return, you know."

"You can't," sighed Silver Bells. "The Great Centaur will never allow it."

"Well, one way or another, we're going to meet again." (*One way or another.* . . . I am not a seer; why did I see for once what the dark should not have disclosed?)

The ladies did not embrace, but at least they exchanged smiles, the friendliest gesture between

79

them since they had met on Bumpers, the hill. My cousin embraced Eunostos, however, as if he belonged to her (recalling her mother, perhaps, my father's sister, in Egypt).

"I wish I had a child like you," she said, and Eunostos cried like a little boy, including the blubbers and snuffles, and Marguerite wiped his nose with the strap of the tunic she wore. Brotherly, Silver Bells took her into his arms and cradled her heart-of-a-daisy hair against his russet chest, and patted her on the back, and—do you know?—the butterfly from the party was circling around his head, and he smiled at her, and it seemed as if she told him to kiss Marguerite on the cheek, for he kissed her and said, "Chiron says that 'parting is such sweet sorrow.' He stole the line and probably got it wrong, but maybe he's right in what he said. We musn't lose the sweetness in the sorrow."

My cousin smiled like a girl who thinks that she hears her father's footstep at the gate—father gone to the war and girl unsure of his safe return, but daring to hope.

"Oryx." He turned to me, and his grave, sweet face was father-brother-and-friend. Would he think me unmanly to hug him? (But I was hungry for family hugs, you see, and I thought, "What the Styx!" and hugged him as if Eunostos' bear had taught me the art, and smelled his rue and felt like a dormouse snug in a hollow tree while a hawk is searching the sky.)

He made a fortress out of his arms.

"Be strong," he said. "But then I know you will. Be safe. And never say good-bye."

When Zoe and I embraced, I did not want a nest or a snuggery; it was *her* I wanted to hold, hoard, protect. I was a rock-girt Mycenaean citadel, and she was the queen I held against pirates and thieves.

Alas, imagination can be a cheat.

"Take care of yourself, boy," she said, gently maternal (and what a passionless kiss!).

"Man," I corrected. "*Seventeen*."

"Beast," she smiled. How could I take offense?

Together we dragged the boat into the cove, dislodging slugs and ants, and Zoe peered at the bottom in case of leaks and Silver Bells turned to the Whinnies who had lurked in the forest to insure our departure.

"Bring my friends an oar," he snapped. "This one is broken." In the time it takes an acorn to fall from a medium oak and roll on the leafy ground and come to rest, one of the Whinnies appeared with a perfect oar (there were better boats in the cove, and hiding places for gear and such).

Smiles instead of goodbyes (at what a cost!), a usable oar, and then we had put to sea, Marguerite and I, in our cockleshell, with Silver Bells calling, "Make due west. You'll find a friendly island. Nothing on it but wild sea birds and a Satyr or two."

But suddenly something—was it a current?—

81

seemed to snatch us across that tranquil bay toward the East, and I heard a cry from Zoe:

"Tritons have got them already!"

And Silver Bells shouted, "Not if I can help it," and lunged in our wake and swam like a dolphin to catch a squid! His hooves made powerful propellants, and soon he had seized our prow and clambered into the boat, his wet red hair a splendor in the sun, his tail upraised like the banner of conquering troops.

A face leered evilly at us from the stern. Seaweed for hair; skin the green of a frog; popped, lidless eyes like those of a blowfish beached on the sand; and of course a slimy tail with barnacles on its tip.

"Arena . . . folk . . . 'ull . . . pay . . . us . . . triple," he said in slow, barely recognizable words. He spoke through sharp, broken teeth; he spoke with a hiss and a threat. If a shark could speak, he would make such a sound.

Silver Bells raised the oar and started to whack the creature's head, but the Triton grinned and the sea erupted with slime and scales, and their owners lifted us bodily out of the water and shook our boat, as a griffin shakes a bird he intends to eat.

"What do they mean?" cried Marguerite. "Arena folk?"

"The Bull Games. They're going to sell us to Cretan fishermen, who will pay them in murex shells and sell us in turn to the masters of the games."

Eunostos and Zoe stood on the shore—to enter

that green and living tide was to sink and drown—
and waved forlorn hands.

The Bull Games. Yes, of course. A Minotaur, a
bull-man, the last adult of his race. What a specta-
cle for the arena, a bull-man against a bull, with
Marguerite and me for the prize!

Chapter Six

Oryx

No sensible man walks within reach of a Triton. If he fails to snatch you with his snaky hand, he swats you with his tail or bites you with his ragged teeth. A typical Triton covets whatever he sees, if only to scrutinize and decide its value to him; if valueless, he will first destroy and then discard. Tritons are children of the sea, which raises storms, sinks vessels, drowns sailors, and sends an occasional tidal wave against the land. The sea is acquisitive, and what it acquires it likes to keep, except in the form of drowned bodies and broken spars and scattered shells. There are exceptions, of course, and just as the sea has sunny moods, so Tritons have even been known to imitate dolphins and rescue drowning mariners. But never count on the sun. . . .

The fishermen—there were four of them in a flat-bottomed, oval boat with cages instead of cabins—were leaning on poles and looking uneasily at the Tritons. Their boat had the innocent look of a platter with three, neatly molded helpings of crushed pulse. Innocence, however, did not require the tall, spiked rail which enclosed the deck and whose doorway was fastened with leather thongs. It was not a fisherman's boat; it was meant to hold or exclude something vastly larger than fish.

Silver Bells, it appeared, was not the only Beast to be captured for barter with Humans, at least from the forested area to which we had sailed in the south. The fishermen must have designed their boat for carrying Beasts to the Masters of the Games, and for trading with dangerous Tritons who, if you did not pay them a price to suit their whims, would seize the would-be trader and flail him to death with their tails. Silver Bells, Marguerite, and I peered from our cockleshell—a head raised too high invited the flip of a tail—and watched the bartering of our fates, and doubtless our lives, between malignant Tritons and avaricious fishermen. Silver Bells crouched between us and enfolded us in a large, protective embrace. His silken-hairy arms were equally gentle and strong. He did not talk; he seemed to sense that his touch was far more comforting to us than words. Furthermore, we were straining to hear what the fishermen said to the Tritons. Having never been sold, we wondered about our value in such a bizarre transaction. If I had been a buyer, I would have paid a fortune for Marguerite or Silver Bells and—dare I confess?—a sizable sum for *me*. To race, to stud, to regale with raunchy tales: such were my arts and skills. Strange, I did not number thievery among the list. *Ah, Zoe Zoe, you are the thief! You have stolen my heart and told me not to steal!*

We were naturally curious and Hermes, we were frightened, Marguerite and I. In our short lives, we had suffered fear and loss, flight and loneliness, but never slavery, the ultimate degradation, not even of the heart (that is to say, until I met Zoe, that undegrading enslaver!).

The spokesman for the Tritons, slapping his tail on the deck, confronted the leader of the fishermen, who possessed a wide, squashed head like a hammerhead shark, and bulging eyes. You had the feeling that one of the eyes might fall to the ground, so insecurely did they seem attached to the head. It is said by the Cretans that the Goddess created wonder and beauty in the world, but her son, a child at the time, had made the terror and ugliness, the fearsome monsters and the monstrous men, just as a human child may scribble Cyclopes on tablets of stone or sheets of papyrus, or model clay into marauding wolves.

They conversed in an all but unintelligible combination of perverted Cretan and the series of hisses and snorts which comprise Tritonian. (Have you ever heard a slave being auctioned on the block? The auctioneer's speech perverts whatever tongue he speaks.) I caught such words as "more," "Bullman," "murex"; there were obvious threats and promises interspersed with scowls and grins (the teeth of a Triton are close-packed and numberless; lost in a fight, they quickly replace themselves;

again the shark. There were hisses which served the Triton for expletives and were understood by the fisherman. At any rate, the bargainers reached an agreement and, for the first time, their smiles—leers I should say—were simultaneous. In exchange for the three of us, the fisherman offered a barrel of murex shells, cleansed and polished and ready for wearing in pendants around the neck. The precious dyes, of course, had been extracted for the robes of kings, and the shells were valueless except to Tritons, who liked the look of them and thought them bringers of luck. The fisherman—Hammerhead, I had started to think of him—was careful, however, not to open the door in his railing and not to venture from the support of his friends, who resembled each other and also well fed squids. Perhaps they had grown to suit their occupation. They shared an odor of fish and filth, and their loin cloths could have been the rags discarded by household slaves. Together the four of them lifted a large cedar beam with a hook on the end and thrust it across the railing and balanced it, quivering, over the Tritons—and us.

"Go," hissed the chief Triton. He bared his teeth in a grin or a snarl. It was the only word he spoke to us.

"Gladly," I snapped, but Silver Bells hushed me with a shake of his head. I had thought to be going from worse to better, from the inhuman (not the *non*-human) to our own, however inimical world. Silver Bells seemed to agree—with reservations—

and did not want me to anger the Tritons into changing their minds.

Marguerite was unceremoniously hooked by her tunic to the beam, lifted into the air, and dropped among the fishermen. The Tritons handled her like a piece of wood. To them, a Human is ugly, and a beautiful woman the ugliest of her race. A reversal, you see, in point of view. Hideous Hammerhead was probably handsome to his friends, or to the Harpies with which the Tritons mate. I gasped at Marguerite's flight, but she lit and sprang to her feet and smiled encouragement to me.

I was less secure in my own transferral; I knew that my tenuous loin cloth, old, torn, rotting, could easily burst and drop me onto the spikes. The wind in my face was cool but comfortless; I could see the boats and their ominous occupants but I could not close my eyes! A mess of maggots seemed to crawl in my stomach and slither up my throat. Then, the jolt of arrival, the rough hands hustling me into a cage beside Marguerite. She pressed my shoulder and broadly smiled.

"We made it, Cousin," she said. "The Mother has smiled on us."

(Strange, we had broken one of our own steadfast rules: "Excessive hope is the food of fools.")

Then it was Silver Bells' turn. Wearing no garments, he had to be trussed to the pole with a piece of line. He somehow survived the trip with dignity and joined us in the cage, erect and proud, a figure of living fire. I marvelled to see that the bells still hung from his horns and felt a premonition from gods or demons: *It is time to despair when Silver Bells loses his bells.*

The walls of the cage were wooden stakes (bamboo, said Silver Bells, brought to the island by Centaurs from the distant East). We could look between them and breathe the fresh sea breeze. Not that we liked what we saw. Or being seen. We were scrutinized as if we were slaves. And of course we were. Or worse.

Still, we dared to hope.

The four fishermen studied us through the walls. I felt like a fish, about to be brained and eaten.

"Ladies 'ull like the lad," said Hammerhead. "Looks right springy too." A nod of agreement. (Perhaps they would sell me as a stud?)

If they glanced at me, they stared at Marguerite. She refused to sit; she stood with regal presence and glared in turn at each of the staring men, and you would have taken her for a Sumerian queen, receiving court. Her beauty had somehow grown instead of diminished in the Country, and, exiled, captured, pinched, prodded, hoofed, and dumped, she had flourished instead of wilted. Still, she was not misnamed for the Marguerite Daisy, the simplest of flowers. Carmine would seem an affront to her rubicund cheeks. A princess, yes, but robed in simplicity.

"Girl's got spunk," said Hammerhead, a trifle cowed. "Ought to sell fast."

And Silver Bells? Well, I expect they had never seen a Minotaur. They commented on the color of his hair; they observed the hardness of his hooves ("hard as a wench or a chain"); they remarked on his horns and shook their heads at the sight of the silver bells.

Then, the tail. . . .

"That good for anything?"

"Swatting thievish sailors," said Silver Bells, with a lash through the bars at the fisherman's foot.

Hammerhead squealed and stooped to nurse his wound.

"Ain't thieves," he pouted. "Paid, we did." They did not retaliate with blows; they did not wish to damage the merchandise.

He and his three friends, looking as if they belonged in the sea, eating each other, perched on the prow of the boat and proceeded to get completely and merrily drunk on cheap malt beer. They seemed to feel that they had happened upon a prodigious piece of luck. The value of Silver Bells was clearly beyond price, and Marguerite had also impressed them with her manner and looks. Even I looked "springy."

"What am I supposed to do?" I asked. "Spring about piping on a flute like a drunken Satyr?"

"And me," said Marguerite with obvious disappointment. "They don't seem to care in the least about my skills. Nobody even asked."

"To outguess a Cretan is to answer a Sphinx's riddle. I know I sound like Chiron, but it's true, and I didn't steal it. All we can do is wait until our captors sober up enough to pole us ashore." He forced a tentative smile. "But remember, Cretans are far from the

cruelest of men. Look to lower Nubia for the killers."
It must have caused him pain to praise the men who
had killed Alyssum. But he wanted to lessen the pain
called fear in Marguerite and me.

"And you, my dear," said Marguerite. She never
spoke with such sweetness except to me. "Did they
hurt you when they tied you to that pole?"

"I'm tough," he said. "Under this silky fur is sheer
muscle." But I saw some blood on the fur and I
thought how his manly race had dwindled and died
because it was their nature to risk their lives in the
defense of their friends and neighbors and even
strangers.

If Pseira was a wonder of octagons, Phaistos was
equally wonderful with squares and rectangles (and
never imagine a stark and symmetrical city in the
Egyptian style). Pseira was a garden of lotuses. Phaistos was a city of colored blocks, built by the God when
he was still a child, and not in a mood to make such
hideous beings as Tritons and Harpies and the monster Sphinx. No two rectangles, no two squares, were
precisely the same size, even though many stood in
pairs or clusters, several sharing a single wall; or perhaps a pygmy square, a single room, perched like a
soldier's helmet atop a titanic base.

Like Pseira, Phaistos mingled blues and reds—blue
facades, and red, bulging columns in the porticoes of
the marketplace and fronting the sometime palace of
the king, Minos XIII, who ruled the island from
Knossos to the north. Like Pseira, it did not have any

temples, those formidable, faultlessly geometrical structures with pylon gates you find near Egyptian tombs; or the halls of megarons of Achaean cities, Mycenae, Sparta, and Athens. The rustic Cretans worship in caves or on mountaintops, the metropolitan Cretans worship in household shrines, where they place an image of ivory or terra cotta—perhaps the Goddess, perhaps her son; perhaps the Divine Bull who holds the island securely atop his shoulders or a pair of horns to symbolize his power. Whether goddess or son, bull or horns, the image will move the worshippers by its smallness and delicacy, not overpower them like an Egyptian pharaoh carved in the side of a cliff.

Phaistos differed from Pseira, however, in its *spirit,* and the spirit resided in more than the shape of its buildings, or the keelless Egyptian vessels, resting along the beach to the West of the town, sails lowered, oars stacked on the decks (I supposed but could not discern). We had not been welcomed in Pseira; we had been arrested, tried by a judge, and sentenced to probable death, a harsh sentence for a minor theft. Still, we had found a sort of justice for a crime which the people of Pseira—indeed, all of mercantile Crete—take with the utmost seriousness. The island depends on trade, merchants, barter; therefore, theft is a heinous crime.

But the spirit of Phaistos was different. In Egypt every city had its patron deity. The patron of Phaistos must be the God as a small boy: handsome, utterly engaging, and totally ruthless in getting his way, even with his mother, the Goddess. *Capricious.* That was the word for him. And his caprices could delight—or destroy. He had created a colorful clutter of a town; he had also made the Harpies, Tritons, and Lamias.

I was not surprised that Phaistos was famous for its annual games, held in his honor, or that their nature changed from year to year or that the date of them changed from month to month. When the god was feeling benign and sharing the mood with his subjects, trained dancers from Knossos frolicked over the backs of raging bulls, and few were lamed and no one was killed, unless he should fail in his leap. Or there were singers who sang of the harvest home and dancers who danced to the jangle of sistrums and actors who performed a pantomine to celebrate creation and the gifts of the Goddess whose most unpredictable gift was her son. If the mood of the son was cruel, then men must die in a variety of ways which only the imaginative Cretans (never the stolid, unimaginative Egyptians) could devise.

This year, who could say? We only knew that the Games would honor the God, and include a bull—and us.

The Cretans, like all of their neighbors on the mainland—Achaeans, Egyptians, Babylonians—import slaves from foreign lands, and slaves must be displayed, bought, and sold, usually in the marketplace among the shops and stalls. I knew that Phaistos had its market and its blocks for display where men and women were stripped and examined—the

men for youth and strength, the women for beauty
and grace.

Silver Bells, Marguerite, and I were not, however,
taken into the town. The attention we had received
was special—and ominous—and we were hardly surprised that our destination was a villa between the
town and the sea. By now it was almost dusk; by now
I was tired to the point of exhaustion, and my ob-
servations were dim to say the least . . . a hedgerow
enclosing a large estate . . . a cluster of coconut
palms achatter with blue monkeys from the jungles
of Libya . . . a pool of blue lotuses . . . and of
course a stone, many-rectangled villa with two levels
and a garden on the roof. (It was said that the Goddess had robed the world in green, herself in blue,
her son in red. "Let there be colors," she said, "and
let them be bright and fortunate, instead of funereal
black and nondescript brown. Brown is for pyramids,
those tombs the Egyptians will build for housing dead
kings. As if they will need a house when they die,
those foolish kings!")

Our captors waited in the vestibule while a slave
went to fetch the master to examine the catch. Hammerhead fretted and swore at the wait; his inarticu-
late friends affixed their faces to their leader's mood.
Meanwhile, two old women came to remove our
sandals and bathe our feet and faces in myrrh; melancholy Libyans, the folk of the South, exiled but not
bereft of their kindliness.

"Mistress," said the elder to Marguerite. Her skin
looked like that of a coconut black from the sea.

"You've nothing to fear. Your youth and your beauty will keep you from menial tasks. But *him*"—she pointed to Silver Bells—"I never saw such a one. Not even in the nethermost jungles of Yam."

The slave returned and ushered us into a room with stone couches running along the walls, and murals of bulls and bull dancers and the symbol of male deity, a pair of golden horns. A table held a rhyton or drinking pitcher in the shape of a bull, and the sacredness of the room was apparent to all of us.

The owner of the villa, a gamemaster by the name of Malos, rich, sleek, respected for his profession, wearing a loin cloth for which he was much too fat, entered the room with the walk of a man who is used to being obeyed. I expected a leer for Marguerite, a phantom of loveliness in the dying light, and I saw that she shared my expectations, but he gave her a quick, admiring nod, dismissed me with a glance, and stared raptly at Silver Bells.

He clapped his hands and squealed and his fat brown stomach quivered above his belt, like the foaming of beer about to overflow its cup.

"A Minotaur! It's true, it's true!"

"*Said* it was," sulked Hammerhead.

Malos examined Silver Bells from his horns to his hooves and listed his attributes:

"Tail's not molted.

"Hair as glossy as silk from the East.

"Horns like antlers, and made from mother of pearl."

"Sir," said Silver Bells in a level voice. "I am not

a bull on the hoof. I am a Beast. True, I am your captive, but if you continue to list my qualities, I will gore you with my 'mother of pearl.' It's hard, by the way."

"Gore me and your friends will feed my griffins." Malos did not shout. He did not even raise his voice in the way of merchants who wish to protest a price.

Silver Bells paused and a terrible anger ruddied his face. He was not accustomed to bland words and cruel intentions.

"Very well," he said. "I will do what you wish. So long as you do not harm my friends."

"Forget about us, Silver Bells," I cried. "It's you they seem to want for their—caprices."

The Gamemaster, not even deigning to recognize my outburst, turned to Hammerhead. "It is not a time to bargain. You have brought me a treasure. Name your price."

"A hundred ingots of copper," said Hammerhead, a moderate sum to Malos, a fortune to fishermen.

"As you wish."

"And the drinkin' pitcher!"

"That too."

Hammerhead and his squids departed with the look of men who have outwitted the "city folk." I feared (hoped?) that he would lose an eye in his enthusiasm.

Malos resumed his scrutiny of Silver Bells. Then to his slaves: "House them, feed them, tend them with care. If they are flawed in any way, especially the Minotaur—"

96

The Cretans sometimes sacrifice a bull to honor the Great Bull who upholds the island. They think it an honor to both the animal and the God and, not having fought a land war in several centuries, they also relish the sight of blood.

My acorn of hope diminished into a seed, and, in spite of myself and my promise to Marguerite, I remembered the past. Like a ravening brute, it shook me in its maw.

Egypt . . . childhood . . . dwarf chrysanthemums, cornflowers, and sycamore figs around a lotus pool with pads as large as elephant ears. I, a manly eleven, loved by parents and cousin Hora (who had lived with us since her family died of the Plague) . . . father a trader, born in Mycenae, settled in Memphis to trade with lands to the south . . . Hora already ripe for marriage and courted by wealthy fathers for stalwart sons. . . .

We played beside the pool, Hora and I; indulgent girl in a white, ankle-length sheath and younger boy, naked and unashamed, head shaved except for the "lock of youth."

"Catch," I cried, as I threw a ball of stitched leather enclosing barley husks.

I did not hear the thud of the ball in my cousin's hands.

I heard the scream, as unexpected as lightning in the time of the Drouth. My mother, that frail and luminous lady whom kings had wooed, stood on the high-roofed veranda and leaned on a column topped by a stone lotus bud. There was blood on her face and robe. Otherwise, she was a white as a pillar of salt—white robe, white face, white hands outstretched as if to thrust us into a safer world. It was she who lingered, almost dead on her feet, in a world which had ordered her into the dusk. Her spirit was poised to fly from her lips. She had stayed its flight to warn us; delayed her burial, journey, joining with Osiris in the Celestial Garden.

"Father dead. Hide. H . . . i . . . d . . . e."

Behind her I saw a bristle of wings, an enormous, feline head, slouching from side to side and dripping blood from its jaws.

"Mother!" I started to run to her help. Or perhaps to seek her help.

"Too late," cried Hora. "The pool—"

"No!"

She seized my hand in a cruel grasp.

"A Sphinx," she said. "Their vision is dim. They follow your scent, which they never forget. The water will hide us, if anything. It's what they hate the most. If they drink it, they die."

We crouched under lotus pads, sucking the thin trapped air, hoping the bulge of our heads would not be seen on the bank.

But we could hear. . . .

The slow, careful pad of the catlike feet as she searched the garden, sniffing the air; uprooting a sycamore fig and hurling the bush to the ground; shaking a palm until the coconuts fell from the fronds. I saw it in my mind; I saw my mother's hands and vomited, endlessly, wrenchingly, somehow stifling sound.

Our villa lay at the edge of the green and irrigated land around the city of Memphis in Upper Egypt. Beyond, the waterless desert. . . . Beyond, the water-despising Sphinxes, older than pyramids, older than men. We kept their little cousins for pets and worshipped a goddess, Bast, in the shape of a cat. But Sphinxes were cats perverted into monsters. In Egypt (perhaps the world?), the land of balance, every virtue has its opposite vice, every friendly animal, its opposite predator. . . .

She reeked of my parents' blood. She breathed with a whining breath which stung my ears like a wasp.

Eternity poised at the side of the pool . . . and tired . . . and returned to the house. It had only killed; now it must feed.

There was nothing left of our family to mummify.

Why did I think of a Sphinx in a Cretan villa awaiting a game with bulls?

Of padding feet and blood?

"Oryx," said Marguerite.

"Yes?"

"You have broken our promise. I can see the memories in your face." She kissed my cheek.

"I'm sorry. Never again."

Never say never. . . .

Chapter Seven

Zoe

I did not waste the time to seek an official audience with the King. Those who wished a favor were expected to follow a circumscribed course, send him a gift, bribe his messenger (who shared the bribe with Chiron), and await his whim—perhaps a day, perhaps a week. He had learned a pharaoh's ways.

I followed Zoe's way. I strode through the fields surrounding his palisade; I trampled cabbages in my haste, demolished hayricks, ignored the patterned beauty of vineyards and olive trees, wine presses bright in brick and water-mills perched over streams like Titans kneeling to drink. Travelers in their youth, settled agriculturalists in their maturity, the race claimed many achievements (except their king), but I had come to seek and not admire. I did not even chaff with the Centaurs at their work, several of them my lovers, who hailed me with a blithe, "Good morning, Zoe."

"I have come to see your king." Terse and abrupt.

Pruning grapes which were soon to be ripe, or shaking the olive trees to gather the green and precious fruit, they paused and watched with alarm and seemed to forgive my haste.

Then the palisade, a thick circular wall of cedar beams, with a gatehouse perched on the wall to the left of the gate, like a bodiless head, the stakes in its lower windows, teeth; its upper oval windows, squinting eyes.

"And whom shall I say is calling?" asked the guard at the gate, a young steed of a fellow, proud in a scarlet jerkin and armed with a bronze-tipped spear.

"You know very well," I snapped. "Or ought to." (I had taught him the facts of life.)

"But it's e-expected," he stammered.

Of course. Expected by Chiron, who liked a show of force by his peaceable race. I had my doubts that the guard could hurl a spear. I gentled my tone but not my urgency.

"Announce that Zoe, the Dryad, has come to call on the King."

"I believe he is meeting with foreign emissaries," he said, with the look of a man who does not like to lie.

"Sleeping off last night's orgy, you mean. Say that Zoe *demands* to be heard."

Let him do his worst, let him impose a *year* of chastity. Because of him and his evil mind, my friends, already captives, would soon be sold as slaves.

He did not take offense; he saw my concern and quickly called to a friend:

"Zoe, the Dryad, requests an audience with his Greatness." Then to me. "And Zoe, may I ask you the reason? He always wants to know. And, uh, have you brought him a suitable gift?" (Suitable meant expensive.)

"The gift must wait. The Tritons have captured Silver Bells."

His long ears quivered and twitched; the question in his face became concern.

"Silver Bells. You don't mean—"

"Yes, I do."

"I'll go myself. Here, Peppercorn. Take my place. Take my spear. Hold it straight now."

"What for?" demanded Peppercorn, a rustic type on his way to the fields with a hoe. "No more wolves. Nothin' to spear."

"Because."

The gatemaster, circumventing various guards and orderlies, led me directly to Chiron's private stall— not the audience chamber in his palace, but the long, lean room where he entertained his mares, whether wives or mistresses, and special friends like Silver Bells. The stall was narrow to let him stand and sleep, leaning against a wall, for Centaurs always stand when they sleep, unless with a two-legged mate. Still, a Centaur is a tremendous Beast, what with his many limbs, and a space which was narrow for him was wide for me. I sat on a six-legged stool with a cushion, stuffed with rushes and prickling through my gown, and tried to order my words. An unlit lantern— daylight shone in the four rectangular windows— swayed its boatshape above my head; boat like a crescent moon, brought from the East. Other Eastern objects adorned a niche in the wall at the opposite end of the room, a dragon of green, veined jade, a screen in miniature, with rose quartz signs and figures, and an incense jar emitting a scent which I would have called a smell. But the charms of the room—even the smell—escaped me on this particular visit. I had visited the stall for happier times and always remembered to compliment Chiron on his *objets d'art.* He was very proud of them; when he added another wife, he always let her choose from his collection: except the dragon of jade.

The time for compliments was yesterday.

I did not address him by title or even name.

"Because of your sentence, Tritons have captured Oryx and Marguerite. And Silver Bells swam after their boat, and *they got him too.*" Chiron had his feelings, in spite of his affectations. His respect for Silver Bells was touchingly real, though envy was mixed with admiration (a king by chance, not merit, mistrusts a kingly friend).

He snorted and stomped his hoof. "Damnable Tritons. Slavers, thieves, murderers. And in *my* kingdom. Or almost." Then, a wistful shake of his mane. "And Silver Bells—they *would* steal him. It's a Minotaur's nature to rescue those in distress. So of course he had to help those troublemakers."

"Silver Bells is hardly typical. He is the *best* of his race. He helped for the sake of friendship and not for duty. And that should be our reason for helping him. One way or another, we have to get him back." I did

not repeat the names of Oryx and Marguerite, who
would not have advanced my case.

"A bribe, do you think? I have my *objets d'art.*
Possibly, I could part with my dragon."

"There is nothing as valuable to them as Silver
Bells. I was thinking of guile. We'll have to go after
him."

"But how can you leave your tree for the time it
will take?" A dryad's dependence on her father tree
increases with her years.

"Three or four days," I said, "before I start to
pine."

"And sicken and die?"

"At least a week. But that should be long enough
to find Silver Bells. If it isn't, we shall have lost him
anyway."

"And of course we'll need a ship, won't we, Zoe?"

"Strong. Ship-shape."

"Alyssum's ship. After all, it brought her from
Egypt. The Tritons can't overturn it, can they?"

Memory can be the flash of a firefly. I remembered
Alyssum's coming. . . .

I was walking with Silver Bells beside the sea. He
liked to compose a poem in his mind or count the
seagulls or gather coquina shells to string for the
Bears of Artemis. And then we saw the diminutive
ship . . . Egyptian. Never intended for the Great
Green Sea. Still, there was a tiny deck house, a sail
the height of Melissa, a till without a tiller, a broken
oar.

Alyssum lay on the deck, hand clutching the oar. Pale, barely conscious, beautiful as—well, there was no one with whom to compare her, she was so much comelier than her sister Naiads. She made *me* look like a common wench. Bluer-than-lazuli hair enwreathed her head, a cushion against the papyrus-deck. Between her toes were the nacreous webs which signified a Naiad. The race had come with the Centaurs from the East, but some had lingered in Egypt, haunting the caves of the Upper Nile and rarely seen by traders or explorers, their habits as secretive as their haunts.

Silver Bells entered the water and lifted the prow of the ship upon the shore and bound it with a line to heavy rock.

"We mustn't move her yet," he said, clambering onto the deck. "Zoe, can you fetch her a posset from your tree? Here, I'll bathe her face with a damp cloth." Lacking a jerkin or loin cloth, he tore the hem from her gown, dipped it into the sea, and stroked it lovingly over her brow.

She opened her eyes. They were almost the color of aquamarines; as haunting and melancholy. ("The heart of the sea," they are called. The fury lies in the storms; the heart in the stones.)

"Tritons," she murmured. "Thought I was dead. Let me drift."

"Where are you from?" asked Silver Bells. His voice would have reassured a frightened child whom woodsmen have rescued from a pack of wolves.

"Egypt," she whispered. "Upper Nile." Her voice was the wind in a coconut frond. "Where am I?"

"Crete."

Her eyes grew wide and afraid. "A storm," she said. "It drove me from the Nile and into the Great Green Sea. Drowned my crew. I had only meant to visit a Human friend in the Delta region."

"Never mind," he said. "We'll get you back to Egypt. Zoe, what about that posset?". . . .

But he fell in love with her and asked her to stay with him and become his bride. Thus, they were married and she was a queen to us. Until her death.

He had kept her ship in a cluster of seagrapes, under a canopy, and painted the hull and repaired the sail even after her death, as if it were one of those funerary boats in Egyptian tombs.

"But you must have protection" said Chiron. "Against the Tritons. Or they will get you too and *do their worst*. The ship is much too small to hold my Whinnies, and as for myself, my duties of state keep me close to the palisade." .

"Eunostos," I said. "Small, but he never misses a bird with his bow. Melissa. Her teeth could make a Triton show his tail. And as many of those Panisci girls—ill-mannered though they are, they do love Silver Bells—as I can crowd on my deck. Their slings can be deadly. And now. There is no time to lose."

"But I haven't dismissed you from my presence!"

"Dismiss me twice when I return from my quest. I'll bring you a *special* gift."

Too much time had already been lost. Beasts who were trapped by Tritons were quickly sold to the Cretan Arena Masters.

The ship sat jauntily under its canvass roof. If a snake or a butterfly can incarnate a soul, why should a ship not epitomize its owner? It was Alyssum's ship which would guide us to Silver Bells (her ship, her spirit, herself). I felt a sunburst of hope.

A failing perhaps, my eternal hopefulness. I have suffered my disappointments. (I have not had children; in all of my lovers I have not found a Silver Bells. Still, I remember the Golden Age. It will come again, it will come again. . . .)

"Eunostos," I cried. "Have you brought your bow?"

"And a quiver of arrows too! We will find my uncle won't we, Aunt Zoe?" His solemn face had lost its smile. His feathered hat, awry, deserved to sit like a crown atop his head.

"Yes, my dear, we will find the three of them. I swear by my father's oak. Now go and fetch the provisions I told you about. And our means of disguise, if it should come to that."

"And Oryx," added Melissa. "Will we save him too? He has stolen my heart and I want to get it back."

"We will save him too." I forced myself to add, "And Marguerite." She wore a chain of coquinas instead of her usual violets, a gift from Silver Bells. But she carried a calyx of honey, a gift for Oryx. "He may be hungry when we find him," she said. Bees and Bear Girls share an affinity. The Bear Girls scout for places to build a nest; the grateful bees are quick to share their honey.

"All right now, you Panisci," I shouted. "Are we going to work together?" Six were the most I could hide in the cabin or crowd aboard the deck. Six were a multitude, six were a mob.

" 'Ear, 'ear," mocked one of the girls. "Are we goin' to work together?" I heard the whirr of a sling and a coconut fell from a distant tree. "Practicin'," she grinned.

I gave her a Gorgon stare. "Why don't you practice for *him?*"

"Cor, if a look could kill. Reckon we are. For 'im, not for 'er."

"Aunt Zoe," asked Eunostos. "Where is my uncle's butterfly?"

"Why, I expect she will follow us when she may," I said.

"Can't. Not over the sea. Well, we shall have to go without her. Will we lose our luck, do you think?"

"We will make our own."

"I'm coming too! Got the whole story from Chiron." Moschus, who else? Bless him, his heart was kind, whatever his weakness for spirituous beverages.

"My dear, you are much too large, but thank you for the thought."

"Large and strong. What's wrong with that?"

"You'll overturn the boat."

"Oh." I saw a tear in his eyes. "What can I do then, Zoe?"

"Drink a libation to Dionysus. Besides his other duties, he's also a guardian of ships."

"Right away!" He hurried to look for a cache.

And so we launched our boat in a dangerous sea, the Whinnies to shove us through the surf, and Chiron to shout encouragement from the beach. Blue sail, red hull, green till and oar. . . . Deckhouse like a bird nest of rushes and stalks of papyrus. Eunostos the tiller, I the oarsman, Melissa the lookout; the Panisci girls our company of marines. A nimble ship, a stout crew, and a purpose stronger than bronze.

"Tritons," I cried. "Stop us if you dare!" Only they could tell us where we must sail. They had seen us leave the beach, and a taunt was the quickest way to get them to show their faces and establish communications. I knew the risk; I also knew the need.

I felt the slap of a tail against the hull, saw the flicker of green as the owner rose on the other side of the boat. Testing. I felt a bump and a nudge, but the *Nilus* held to her course.

"We aren't a cockleshell," I laughed. "You can't sink us and you can't stop us. I suggest you talk."

A Triton clambered over the gunwale and faced Eunostos' bow, aimed to kill.

"Sir, did you hear my aunt? She asked you to talk. Politely."

"Got friends," he hissed.

Whoosh, went Melissa's sling and a friend took a sudden dive.

"What do you want?" inquired our first invader, switching from words to Tritonian hisses. Fortunately, I understood his tongue.

"What have you done with Silver Bells?"

"Who?"

He was playing ignorance, plotting mischief.

"Eunostos," I said, "I believe he needs a lesson."

The bow tautened. The little-boy hands seemed scarcely able to restrain the arrow.

"The bull-man with bells on his horns," I amplified.

"Oh, him. Why should I answer *you*?"

"If you don't, you and your friend—the one who is trying to creep onto the bow—will feel the bite of Eunostos' arrows before you can even dive."

"That *boy*?"

"That boy is Silver Bells' Nephew."

"Ummmmm." He had to weigh and deliberate. Thought comes hard to a Triton. He had to measure the speed of a dive against the flight of an arrow. His stupid yellow eyes held glints of craft but also shadows of fear. An arrow in his tail, his pride, his propellant! The prospect gave him pause. At last. "Sold him, we did. Others too."

"To whom?"

He shrugged. "Fishermen. Look the same to me."

"Why?"

"For murex shells. Want to see?"

"I mean, why did the fishermen buy them?"

"Games."

"Where? In Knossos?"

"Phaistos." The name made me feel as if a rat had started to climb my back. The games of Knossos were gaudy but rarely cruel. The games of Phaistos ranged from merry to barbarous. Phaistos was not so civilized as larger, northern Knossos. It fronted Libya, the Sphinx-haunted deserts, and below them, the pygmies of Nubia who tipped their darts with slivers of human skulls.

"You are a bloody murderer," I snapped.

"Trader," he shrugged. His grin was a glitter of shark-ragged teeth. He was doubtless thinking of murex shells. "Go now?"

"Yes. I never want to see you again."

"Tell him to lower his bow."

"Once you have dived. You will have to trust him."

"Trust?"

"You don't know the word, do you? Learn it then."

He scowled and dived and Eunostos lowered his bow and ran to my side.

"What shall we do now, Aunt Zoe?"

"You have already been a hero," I smiled, hugging him to my breast. (I wanted to keep him a child; I wanted to stop that impossible meddler, time, and be forever his "aunt." I have never been one afraid of change. But something gave me pause, and more than the growth of Eunostos from child to man. Change had seemed in the past the Sphinx of Achaea, mysterious rather than evil; maker of riddles for me to solve. Change had become the evil Sphinx of Egypt, insatiable to kill; the "desert shark.") "Are you still feeling heroic?"

"More. I've practiced, don't you see. I was scared before."

"So was I."

"You, Aunt Zoe?"

"Only fools are fearless on such a mission."

Our course was clear: We must sail to Phaistos and somehow contrive to rescue our friends from the Cretans; worse, from the Games.

"What shall we do then, Aunt Zoe?"

"Keep sailing," I said. "Toward Phaistos."

"But they'll capture us too!" A Goat Girl wailed, and winced when Melissa bit her scraggly tail.

"Let Aunt Zoe finish. I'm sure she has a plan."

I seemed to hear the tinkling of faraway bells. The kind, grave face appeared in the eye of my mind. (I seemed to hear, "I love you, Zoe, friend, rescuer, *woman* to make me forget my lost Alyssum." Ah, foolish, foolish . . . Even the hopeful must limit hope.)

"Yes, I have a plan."

Disguise.

Chapter Eight

Zoe

In the late afternoon, when the sun seemed an ox-cart instead of a fiery chariot, we beached our boat beside a murky stream. (Nobody sails at night except a fool or a seasoned mariner and even he avoids the winter seas.) I had carefully chosen the stream because its darkness suggested the presence of umber in its banks. Behind us, sea-grapes rose into uplands where carob tree mingled with palm; before us, the water stretched shipless and calm and islandless; above us, strange, funnel-shaped clouds shifted and intermingled but spilled no rain.

Before the falling of dusk, I fastened a pennant from the bow: murex purple, inscribed with a golden lion; a gift from my Nubian lover. (He had given me further gifts: a knowledge of his language, his customs, his land. The amount one can learn in the couch is limitless. I have had less success with scrolls, which give me a headache or redden my eyes.)

"Dig where?" asked Melissa, ready to pout. "I don't want to soil my fur."

"The stream," I said. "There's umber above the

beach. Shovel it into a pigskin—see, I have taken the skins from which we have drunk our wine and split them down the top—and bring it aboard the *Nilus.* Here. Use this lantern. It's getting dark. Otherwise, you can't tell umber from earth."

"You won't tell us your plan, Aunt Zoe?" asked Eunostos. Sadness had left him when we had started our mission; he trusted in me to find his uncle. Now, he mingled a man's gravity with a child's curiosity.

"Not yet," I said, assuming the look of a mother who knows a secret. For the sake of the children, I wanted to lessen the fear in a fearful voyage. And to a child, a secret is likely to tantalize instead of terrify. "If I can surprise you, I can surprise the Cretans."

"Kid games," the Goat Girls snickered. They still looked identical except in height, though Silver Bells claimed to have noticed variations in the contours of a hoof, the length of a tail (minute at best), even in manners and mood. The speaker, I judged from her tone, was that inveterate troublemaker, Hensbane, one of the band who had waylaid Oryx and Marguerite on Bumpers, the hill.

"Deadly games," I corrected. "Continual jeopardy." It seemed, after all, that I must emphasize fear.

"Deadly games," murmured Phlebas, savoring both of the words as if they were morsels of cuttle-fish. It was his first adventure. Imagination, it seemed, had proved at best a tolerable substitute. Reality intoxicated him like dogberry beer. If only he were as slender and short as Eunostos! Because of his size, he

114

complicated my plan. "Jeopardy. Does that mean danger, Zoe?"

"Of the worst kind."

"I expect we shall all be captured but make a daring escape from jeopardy and—"

"Enough, Phlebas. You don't have to pretend. You're *here*."

(". . . and rescue Silver Bells and win immortal renown and. . . .")

"Umber," groaned Melissa, thinking no doubt of soiling her fur. "I think I hear a bear in the woods."

"Nonsense. There are no bears in these parts." (For all I knew, there might be a wolf or a Cyclops.) "Now do as I say and you shall hear a *part* of my plan" (the only part I had planned, I will have to confess). "Nubian ladies wear voluminous gowns against the heat. Only your face and feet and Melissa's paws will show. Tomorrow, when the umber has dried, you shall stain them a dusky brown—*not* your fur—and pass for my attendants. A Nubian princess is attended by pygmies, you know." (I was going to have a problem with Phlebas. Fat, taller than most of his race, he looked like an adolescent Satyr, not a pygmy. Perhaps my royal jester?) "And cover your ears with one of those hoods they wear. En route, I have stitched one for all of us."

"Do men wear hoods?" asked Eunostos. "They'll make us look like mourners."

"For you a hat." I had made him a rounded cap and fastened an ostrich feather in the brim. Except for hiding the tips of his pointed ears, it was like the cap which his uncle had made for him (with help from me). He thanked me with more than usual courtesy and looked in the stream to straighten the feather to its jauntiest angle. In so many ways he was wise beyond his years that I needed such reminders of his youth.

"What about our 'ooves?" a Goat Girl asked (Bindweed, I think).

"Pigskin boots. The pygmies of Nubia use the antelope's hide, but no one will notice the texture through the dye. Besides, it isn't often that Nubians visit Crete. One can always claim a change in style."

"And what about paws?" Melissa demanded, as if she had posed the insoluble problem. (I think she resented the umber on her fur.)

"Nothing. You'll be an ally from a neighboring tribe. The paws will make you exotic. I expect a Cretan may want to marry you."

"I'm saving myself for Oryx."

"Zoe, your secret is out," blurted Phlebas. "We're going to Phaistos disguised as Nubians. Killers from the south, I suppose?" Nubia is a divided land; the northern area of the merchant princes; the southern jungles of lions and spear-throwing savages.

"Our pygmies are from the south. The Queen and her royal jester from the north."

"Merchants then." Disappointment muffled his voice.

"Merchants, my dear? Queens may engage in trade, but merchants they are not, and you in my retinue will attend to my person and not my figures."

116

"But the boat is Egyptian," remarked Eunostos. "No keel. Bundled papyrus reeds for the deck. . . ."

"Since Nubians don't build seaworthy boats of their own, they buy or steal from Egypt. I have already changed the pennant."

"Aunt Zoe, you think of everything. And thus we'll make our way into—why, into the palace itself, where else? And learn what we need to know about Uncle Silver Bells."

"Clever Eunostos. Now we must work on our plan. I hardly need tell you how to attend. But the Girls will need some practice. Line up now."

"Cor!"

"Hush, you chattering magpie." (Hensbane, who else?) "Need I remind you that three lives are at stake, and one of them *his*?"

I might have invoked the secret name of the Goddess. A stillness fell upon them like a net; as if coerced by its strands, they moved into place and looked to me, the fisherman, to dispose of them.

"There now, you are reasonably straight. If a Cretan minister approaches to greet me, bow. In unison. Practice now. Hand to your tummy, shoulders straight. Remember a bow is not a stoop or a slouch. It must be executed with dignity."

"Don't bow to nobody, lady." Hensbane.

"Call me 'Zoe' in private. 'Mistress' once we reach Phaistos. Ladies have no fun."

"Nobody," echoed Bindweed, another girl from the original gang.

"Bow as I say or find yourself left on the beach. Or

thrown to the Tritons. Of course they will do their worst."

"Wouldn't mind if they done their best."

"Who said that?"

Silence.

"They are also cannibals once they have had their way."

The girls began to practice without demur; Hensbane fell to the ground and rose and mastered a graceful bow.

"Learn fast, eh," she boasted. "All right, girls. 'Ere's 'ow it's done. Bindweed, 'ear what I said."

"Aye."

"Keep it up until you are perfect," I said. "Phlebas, you too." Unfortunately, his stomach intervened in his bow. "A tilt will have to do. But mind you, do it with style. And Melissa, you shall walk on my left, a little behind me, and carry my parasol. Eunostos, you shall carry a spear and clear the way for me."

"Perhaps a bow?"

"A spear. The Nubians haven't mastered the bow."

"Uncle Silver Bells never taught me to use a spear."

"Then you must teach yourself and make him proud of you." I had no doubt of his abilities: he would learn to march and hold a spear and never lower the tip except in an exercise. Given time, he would learn to throw with speed and accuracy.

"And what about me?" asked Phlebas.

"I've already designated you my court jester."

"But what do I do?"

"Jest."

"Just what?"

Of course! He did not know the word. He probably thought that he was a Grand Vizier. I must think of a way to make him my jester without wounding his pride and without taxing his modest abilities. "You know. Sing. A royal jester is also a royal bard. I shall make you a pointed cap from a tiger's tail, with a bell on the end."

"Like Silver Bells!"

"Exactly."

"And a tiger's tail too." (The gown I had made for myself would have to forego an extremity.)

"And you shall tell stories as well as sing. Of epic events."

"I know one now. There was this Cyclops, see, and—"

"Once we assume disguise and reach our goal."

The night was silent and chilly; the air was sweet with ripening carob pods. In spite of flintstones aboard the ship, we did not dare a fire, for fear of attracting whatever Humans or Beasts might live in the woods. Bears I doubted, but wolves? Harpies? Sphinxes returned from Libya to Crete, their original home? Civilization on Crete adheres to the coast, or thrives in pockets, as in the Country, divided by ridges and forests.

The cabin was much too small for the whole of the crew, and I did not think it fitting for me to leave my companions and seek a private nest, in spite of my royal estate. Better to stay with them, a queen with her subjects, and see to their courage for the coming trials. Dissatisfaction, it seemed, had come with the dark.

"Wisht I had me a broiled mullet." Hensbane. "What do we get? Curds."

"And dogberry beer," I added, "and carob pods, fresh from the trees."

"Too many seeds."

"If you must have a mullet, throw a line in the water and see what you catch. You'll have to eat him raw, of course."

"Wisht I hadn't come."

"Not even for *him*?"

"Not for that boy and 'is cousin. Snobby 'e was, wasn't 'e, Bindweed?"

"Aye."

" 'Er too. 'Orrible 'air she 'ad. Silver Bells? Like him right well, I do, but—" A Goat Girl's devotion, it seemed, had definite limitations.

"Look," I said. "The star birds are climbing the sky. Silver Bells wrote a poem about them. He always said that Alyssum was more like a bird than a flower."

"Sing us a song, Aunt Zoe," asked Eunostos. "You'll bring us cheer."

Wise little chap, he hoped that a song would enspirit the wavering Girls and remind them of their purpose to rescue Silver Bells, Oryx, and Marguerite.

"I wonder if I can remember—" (I remembered every word, but Eunostos needed distraction as well as the Girls.)

"I'll help," he volunteered.

"Splendid."

"I helped him compose it, you know."

"No, I didn't." (Perhaps I should choose a different poem.)

"In fact, the second line is mine. Some at least. The owl part."

"Very well, but we must watch our voices. I'm used to drinking songs, and we mustn't be overheard." I sang as quietly as the breeze in the mast of our boat, leaving deliberate gaps, and Eunostos filled them with his sweet, child's voice:

The Star Birds

Among the fierce black opals of the dark,
That horned and snowy-feather owl, the moon,
Blue Rigel, fisher in a sky lagoon,
Aldebaran, the stellar meadowlark,
And orange Arcturus, oriole of night
(Fluting what songs to what celestial ears?)
Ascend and in their incandescent flight
Provoke the shaken music of the spheres.

" 'E wrote it, did 'e?" asked Hensbane. After digging the umber, she had washed in the stream and killed her smell of goat. A mischievous girl, she had always seemed to possess only half of a heart, but half, which is more than a Triton or Sphinx can claim, may grow into a whole. (Children, except for rarities like Eunostos, are born without any hearts. They grow them along with their bodies. Some of them grow an acorn, some a coconut.)

"Yes. For Alyssum."

"Never liked pomes. Don't un'erstand 'em. Right takin', though, this one. Think we'll find him, Zoe?"

"At least we shall get into the palace and find out where he is."

"What if they already held them games?"

"Unlikely, so soon." Immediate rescue, nevertheless, was vital for all of us. Our umber stains, applied in the morning before we sailed for Phaistos, would eventually start to run, and I had a further reason to fear delay. I had already started to miss my father tree; I wanted to touch his bark, embrace him as if he were a Beast, bury my face among his feathery leaves; and I knew that my longing reflected a physical need, hardly perceptible, but sure to worsen, soon to kill.

"Sleep now, Girls, and you too, Eunostos and Phlebas. We shall need all our wiles and strength tomorrow."

"Aunt Zoe," said Eunostos. "If we don't find him, the Country will have lost its soul, won't it? It can never become a butterfly or a snake." Then, a little boy, who inevitably sees things small and personal. "And I shall have lost my uncle. Who will teach me to draw a stouter bow? Or write a longer poem?"

"I know what you mean," I said, kissing him on the cheek. "Silver Bells has protected all of us. But if anything happens to him, I promise you this—he *will* return as a snake."

"And still be my uncle?"

"Of course."

"I like snakes."

I held him against me and felt him sink into sleep. "Zoe," said Phlebas. "May I have a kiss?"

The city of Phaistos, set on a hill perhaps a mile from the sea, seemed one twinkling, rainbow-shell facade. The inevitable blues and reds were intermingled with saffron from the crocuses of Egypt. The many-storied palace rose above the law court and other buildings, like a crown on the head of a king who walks fearlessly among his people. Thoroughfares ran to the port, and two-wheeled wagons, drawn by oxen and driven by rustics in loin cloths, carried the produce between the port and the city. From the port came local products like squids and cuttlefish and murex dye; imports like the exquisite linens from Egyptian looms, headbands, alabaster, Nubian gold, papyrus, saffron dye, silver, ostrich eggs, and a new animal called a "horse," a sort of Centaur with only four limbs and a muzzle instead of a face (ugly thing! A caricature of Moschus); from city to port went images carved of ivory, faience cups as breakable as the shell of a peahen egg, daggers with hilts of hammered gold, blue monkeys raised in captivity for export to the ladies of Egypt.

The port was little more than a manifold berth for ships. No fortress withheld it from foreign invasion (for who would risk the wrath of the Cretan fleet?). No pharos beaconed to ships in the dark (for they were beached by dusk or, if caught at sea, they did not need to avoid any shoals on this particular coast.) No vast warehouses—only buildings of brick—stored the merchandise unloaded from deck or hold on the backs of slaves. But what an aviary of ships! Some sat in the water like resting pelicans. Others occupied narrow channels cut into the beach and lined with stones, where a ship might shelter against the severest storm, since the mouths of the channels could quickly be closed with swinging, wooden gates. Sailors were almost the same in every port (or so I was told by a sailor, once my lover), and these, Egyptian, Achaean, Cretan, were sunburned young men with broad, naked shoulders (slender if Cretan) who laughed and joked and exchanged some choice oaths which seemed to be instantly recognizable in any tongue. Nothing shocks me—I can swear with the best of men—but I feared for Melissa's ears. However, she did not appear to understand the oaths. The Bears of Artemis never reach the point where the facts of life are more than a mere abstraction to them. The Goat Girls, however, though equally ignorant, chaffed with the sailors and even swore with them. Many Nubians speak the Cretan tongue, but with an unmistakable intonation, like the rustle of rain in a baobob tree, and I had to hush them before they revealed their disguise.

"We've arrived," I said. "Begun our adventure at last. Don't give us away. Now then."

I ensconced myself in a couch which the Goat Girls had set on the deck and assumed my role as a queen of the South. Eunostos fanned me with an ostrich feather which tickled my nose (but southern queens are not expected to sneeze). Wearing a loin cloth of leopard skin, his reddish chest and limbs disguised with umber, he made a perfect pygmy from the jungles of Nubia. He managed to imitate the savage look of the race and glared at sailors who leered or beckoned at me (not that I minded a *decorous* leer). Melissa and the Goat Girls, similarly dressed and stained, could also pass for pygmies, and, if I carried my part, who could deny that I was a Nubian queen with my retinue, come to consider trade with the merchant princes of Phaistos?

If I carried my part, along with Phlebas, rehearsing a story under his breath. . . .

"Ho, there, my good man," I called to a nautical sort who squatted on one of the wharves and peered at the sea, as if he would rather squat than work. Young but weathered and brown, he had seen the world, so it seemed, and the sight had left him langorous and tired. "Is this berth occupied?"

"Depends." His massive knuckled resembled a sailor's knots. He had worked in his day; now he wanted to rest.

"Well then, give us a hand."

"Cost you."

"Sir, I am a Nubian queen. You are doubtless aware that the chief exports of my country are gold and *hired assassins.*"

He leaped to his feet while I continued to lounge.

In the blink of a falling star, we were moored to the berth.

"Eunostos," I said. "Give the man his reward." Eunostos fetched a casket out of the cabin, loosened the chain, raised the lid, and extracted a large golden elephant with eyes of jade—worth a dozen berths—and solemnly handed it to the nautical sort.

The sailor knew his goods. He gasped and grinned at me. Before we could stop him, he had sprung on the deck and offered his hand to help me to my feet.

I waved him away from my couch with a hint of dismay.

"Don't touch me, my man. My person is sacrosanct. However, I do appreciate your thought." I rose, unassisted, to my queenliest height and stood on the deck to be admired in my Nubian finery. It was not an easy rise, so laden I was with ivory bracelets, golden anklets, earrings as big as goose eggs, not to speak of a tiger skin robe without a tail. Then, preceded by Eunostos with his spear—he held it perfectly straight—followed by Melissa and Phlebas, and flanked by my escort of Goat Girls in a row so precise as to make me proud, disembarked from our vessel and confronted the Enemy.

It was not a time to deliberate; it was a time to act.

"Eunostos, fetch me a carrying chair." (Loudly.) *"Something suitable to my royal person."* Carrying chairs were numerous and various because of the ladies who came to the port to buy fish or imported vegetables—Cretan ladies go anywhere—or travelers from the sea, whether merchant, soldier, wanderer, courtesan, or thief. I dismissed the first three pairs of carriers because their chairs did not look suitable to a foreign queen. The fourth was freshly painted, softly cushioned, brightly canopied against the torrid sun.

"This will do," I said, and I mounted the chair as if it were an elephant in my native land, and, my escort following me on foot, headed for the city and the quest.

"A caravanserai?" inquired my carriers, Libyans both of them, dark, soft-spoken, clearly in awe of me, a Nubian, from a richer, remoter, harder race.

"The palace," I instructed. The King, I assumed (and hoped), was not in residence, though even a king would not force a change in plan. "To seek audience with the Prince!" he cried with growing respect. Prince? He could only refer to Minos' son and heir to the throne, a young man who, being unwed among a people customarily wed at Oryx's age, and who, being both rich and titled, was courted and coveted by every single female on the island. (I had also heard that he was a simpleton.)

"Audience?" I said. "I am *expected*." Did I not have a way with young men? I would use my craft on the Prince to learn what I wished to know. I would ask with disdain why no one had met my ship. I would speak of messages sent and lost. I would speak of gold and slaves and elephant tusks . . . contracts inscribed on stone or written on scrolls and sealed with signet rings.

That is to say, if the sun did not melt the umber on the cheeks of my escort, trudging in the sun.

That is to say, if no one, including myself in my

somewhat jostling course, should lose a hood and prickle with pointed ears.

It is good to expect the unexpected. But "If" has never dominated my life.

I did not doubt that we would find Silver Bells. I did not doubt. . . .

"Just in time for the Games tomorrow."

"Games? What games?"

The first carrier, wiry and small, more like a Blue Monkey than a man, peered over his shoulder with revelations perched on his tongue.

"The Bull Games."

"And what is their nature this year?"

"Nobody *ever* knows, except the gamemasters. But one thing everybody knows."

"And what is that, my man?"

"There's more than a bull this year."

My heart leaped in my breast like a hooked carp. "And what is more than a bull?"

"A bull-man. A Minotaur. And a boy and a lady with yellow hair. And—"

"Please," I said. "My head is about to burst. The sea, don't you know, and now this ride." I must think, I must plan. . . .

"Well now," said the carrier, squinting ahead of us. "The Prince himself is coming to meet you, it seems. See? Purple canopy. Ivory handles. Achaean escort. . . ."

My head had cleared. I had completed my plan.

"Carrier," I said. "You may set my chair in the road. The *middle*."

Thomas Burnett Swann

"And block the Prince's path?"

"Do as I say."

I stepped from the chair and faced the approaching Prince. (*Zoe, summon your wiliest wiles.*)

Chapter Nine

Oryx

"The wine is from Thera," said Marguerite, moving the vessel to the light and judging the color of ripe pomegranate, sniffing the fine bouquet, and touching the brim to her lips.

"The best," said Silver Bells.

"And probably the last," I sighed. "Like the parrot-fish we're eating. Tender and succulent. Spiced with pumpkin seeds. They feed us well. They hold us in this villa which might be a guest house for friends of the fat old man."

The room was sparse but rare with furnishings. We sat at a six-legged table on leather-padded stools. A chair of citron wood, costly and frail, invited the guest to look but not to rest and pervaded the room with its sweet-and-acrid accent. The usual couch of stone, cushioned with pillows in the shape of pheasants, offered to hold the weight of even our host. A small, boat-like brazier promised warmth for evenings in the winter, when snow fell on the mountains and even the coast was ablaze with nocturnal fires.

"Because it isn't for long, you see," I continued.

"Isn't that right, Silver Bells?" In the dark beyond our candles, our snug and substantial walls, I heard the cry of a griffin, shrill and cruel; and distant, tantalizing with thoughts of escape and freedom, the slow reverberation of the sea. (I thought of Tritons to hush my wanderlust.)

He had tried to cheer us since we had left the Country. At such a time, however, he could not bring himself to invent a lie. Whatever words he had said, his grave and tender face would have told the truth.

"Yes. I expect it will be tomorrow."

"Silver Bells?"

"Yes, Sweet Marguerite?"

"I want you to know that—that whatever happens, I will always be Marguerite. The name *you* gave me and never Hora." She somehow restrained her tears, but her eyes were red. She had forgotten a courtesan's way to weep.

"It suited you from the first," he smiled, "though you didn't suspect. And it's grown to suit you more." He drew us into a long embrace, and his hug was the light of a pharos to a floundering ship, a wall against a Sphinx. (But a ship may sink in spite of the light, and a Sphinx may breach a wall.)

"I wish," I began.

"Yes, Oryx?"

"May I keep your name for me?" It was not the question which urged to be asked.

"Of course! Swift as an oryx, stalwart and proud."

"Have you room for a little brother?" I blurted.

"Room for a *younger* brother. Not so little, though. Discounting my horns, you're just about my height."

"I don't want to be your *sister*," cried Marguerite, and, embarrassed, she emptied her cup and began to chatter of trivialities.

"How do the Cretans make their leather?" she asked, pretending to note the stool on which she sat.

I knew how she hurt. Thanks to Zoe, I knew how she hurt and tried to add to the trifles. "From the bulls they sacrifice, I expect." At such a time, I could hardly have made a clumsier try.

I did not expect to sleep that ominous night. And yet I slept before I had finished the parrot-fish and come to the pumpkin slices; I laid my head on the table and dreamed of Zoe giving an orgy for me instead of Chiron.

Slowly I lifted my head and opened my eyes. Roseate morning blinked in the windows.

"Mar—" I began. A simple name was difficult to speak.

"Marguerite." Complete but hushed. We had been drugged, of course. The wine or the parrot-fish.

She drowsed beside me, her hair spilled goldenly over the table like rare ambrosial wine.

I forced an exclamation into my voice. "They have taken Silver Bells!"

"I feel so rested," she murmured, lifting her head. "See, the sun is high in the sky—*Silver Bells gone, you say?*" She tried to leap to her feet, stumbled, and tottered into my arms. I eased her onto a stool. "Dear Hora, they have taken him from us while we slept!"

"Opium juices, wouldn't you say?"

"Mixed with the wine, no doubt. They wanted to keep us quiet. We might have fought when they took him away."

"*Would* have fought." Yes, and killed, and even died for him.

"They wanted to rest us from our capture. They mean us to look our best for the bloodthirsty crowds. You know how they pride themselves on their looks. Even their prisoners have to please their eye!"

"Well!" I muttered. "I'm rested all right. Enough for a fight to the death. Am I looking my best?"

"A trifle dingy, perhaps. Here, there's a smudge on your cheek."

Quietly as an ibex in feather-grass, the Libyans entered the room: the dark old woman with the single eye, a boy and a girl of perhaps my own age with faces meant to be blithe but saddened by their lot, and sad of expression now; surely, sympathetically, they moved among us and saw to our needs. They seemed to walk in peace. Or resignation? I wonder if anyone forgets the land of his birth.

"Mistress and Master," the woman said with surprising forcefulness. It was her subject which gave her spirit—and fear. "We must prepare you for the Games. Master must wear a loin cloth, and a golden bull to hang around his neck, and an armlet of copper embedded with malachite. He must dress like a prince. He must suit the occasion. Mistress must wear. . . .". She paused and seemed to think of a happier time, for herself and Marguerite.

We submitted ourselves to their kind, insistent hands. To fight them would have been useless as well as cruel. We knew of the guards who patrolled the grounds, the guardian griffins, quick to scream and attack. They bathed us separately in a gypsum tub and dried us with myrrh-scented robes.

"Here," said the boy with a grin. He gave me a loin cloth which, I thought, was surely meant for a child, so tight and constricting it felt to my loins, and the metal ring which he hooked around my waist was as cruel as an octopus clasp.

"I am not a Cretan," I coughed. "You will choke me to death."

"Nor is my master plump like me. Let him suck in his breath. There. A little more. Splendid, splendid!" He summoned the girl and both of them, stocky and thick, gazed with admiration at my imprisoned waist.

"Now, can Master still speak?"

"Yes. In a whisper."

"He will soon grow used to his belt. It is a sign of —importance." (Ambiguous word!) "Here." He gave me a mirror of oval bronze. I will have to say that I preened at the "prince" I saw, impossibly slim, his nudity broken only by loin cloth (which covered the loins and left the rest to view), snake-twining armlet, and golden bull of a pendant; hair combed long behind his head and as smooth as spider silk. Really, I am a terrible exhibitionist. With Silver Bells, undress is a matter of custom, with me it is choice. A man is patterned after the Goddess' son and meant to be admired, just as a woman, who reflects the Goddess. If the hordes must stare, they could stare at the most of me and surmise the rest. I was given two gifts, my body and my craft. Zoe, delectable thief, had stolen my craft!

"Does the ring still pinch?" asked the boy.

"To tell the truth," I said, "I might wear a smaller ring."

But Marguerite! She was an image of gold. She wore a saffron, bell-shaped skirt, its hem embroidered with cobalt-blue bulls. Her flounced sleeves were a deeper blue to deepen the blue of her eyes. Her breasts were bare and the nipples were painted gold. Her hair was swept in a swirl behind her head, except that little curls were allowed to tumble above her ears, artless art, the specialty of the Cretans. Her luminescent eyes did not require any kohl; a dash of carmine had reddened her lips. An image, I say, rare and sad and mute. She seemed to be chiselled from ivory and gold—chryselephantine—and now she longed to return to shapelessness, the swift oblivion of inanimate things (but then, were inanimate things oblivious on this island? In any land? I thought of Bumpers, the hill . . .).

"Ah," gasped the girl. "I had taken you for the Goddess."

"No," said the woman, shaking her head with the slow, deliberate movement of the old. Her single eye was not deceived. "The Lady is sometimes grieved for the sake of her children. But she does not fly from her grief."

"I have no wings to fly," said Marguerite. "I wish I had. For Silver Bells is gone."

"Find him." Proudly they left the room, the woman, the boy, and the girl, and left us to ponder the parting admonition.

"Find him?" cried Marguerite. "When I am a prisoner and he is—who can say where?"

"I think," I began. "I think she meant in another way. But of course you've already started."

We were led from the house by two impassive guards, Achaeans instead of Libyans, each of them clad in an apron-like garment which fell to his knees, showing, however, his thighs, and holding a spear with military precision. At the gate, we ascended a chariot drawn by two of those curious creatures, horses, their manes divided into three meticulous tufts—I did not like their odor; I did not like them because they seemed to be Chirons without human faces.

We never saw the Master of the house.

The street we rode was almost peopleless: The people had gone to the Games. An old dotard knelt on a roof and shook his head in wordless sympathy. A small boy, carving a griffin from a pomegranate rind, peered at us through an open door. Otherwise, we confronted clay facades, newly painted, doors rimmed in wood, windows closed with pale yellow parchment against the heat; shops with counters and overhanging roofs; apartments of many levels and few openings, and gardens atop them like shaggy parasols; a drainage canal on either side of the street. A city of shades it seemed, timeless, unused, unworn. Thus the immaculateness of the Cretans, who would sooner beat a slave than litter their streets; thus, a people deathly afraid of dirt but addicted to games where death is expected and cheered.

Near the arena we overtook the stragglers from the crowd and our guards revealed their power.

"Step to the side," they said, simultaneous in command, and one of them prodded a bystander with his spear and cleared a path for us. Achaeans make the best of mercenaries. At ease with weapons, shortsword, ax, or spear, they do not hesitate to kill. (A Cretan would rather *give* an order to kill; he may like the look of blood but not on his hands. It is part of his cleanliness.) And how the obeyers stared at us who would play in their Games! Well, I stared at *them*. Such a small and delicate folk! Handsome, yes, flawlessly made, but I looked with scorn at their black and filleted hair and raised my head to its fullest height to let them see and covet my spider-silken gold!

Then, the Theatral Area, a bee-hive of stone from the distance; an arena close at hand.

"Marguerite," I said, "it isn't as large as I thought."

"You're used to Egypt," she said. "If they had such games, if they had such arenas, they would be large enough to enclose a pyramid. Think in miniature. In the case of such little people, the whole city can crowd

138

into the place." Other races enjoyed other amusements; theatral areas belonged to Crete.

"And most of them have."

Surrounded by such a clamoring multitude, I felt as if I were miniaturized into an ivory figurine like those which the Cretans place in the niche of a household shrine but not, alas, with the spirit of deity. Far from worshipped, I might be lifted and dropped and shattered into a hundred graceless bits.

"Adrift," muttered Marguerite, who was suffering different but no more hopeful thoughts. "Adrift in a maelstrom without a boat."

No, the ring held a dais uncannily shaped like a boat, festooned with crimson streamers, mounted by stairs, surmounted with one cedar pole which flaunted a purple flag. It had the look of an altar as well as a boat (an Egyptian funerary barque for carrying the dead to the place of burial?). Did it offer a voyage of hope or desolation?

Our guards, never breaking their military stance, pointed the way to the steps. One of them, blonde like me but with eyes like solidified lava, announced to us—and the mob:

"Our guests will mount the dais."

Guests. . . . In a curious way, he was right: housed in a villa, fed like favored friends, escorted through the crowd. From the first, our status had been ambiguous but somehow—honorable. We were part of the Games. Of course, we might also be part of a sacrifice. Curious Cretans, cruel without even recognizing cruelty, reverent of the animal whom they sacrificed to their god. In Egypt we had found a similar faith: The deadly crocodile was hunted and killed —and mummified as a god. Superstition? The Beasts had begun to teach us the truth. *Zoe, Zoe, why did you start what you could not finish, waken what should have slept?*

"We have company," I said. An image of the God, molded in terra cotta and wreathed in irises, stood at the head of the stairs like a kindly host.

"Well, he isn't a child," said Marguerite. "He's a young man. He ought to act his age and protect his guests."

"He does as he must," I shrugged. "Remember, the Cretans think if they sacrifice you, your spirit will go at once to the Celestial Garden."

"That's Egyptian. And Osiris judges you first."

"Achaean, Egyptian, Cretan—we're such mongrels, Cousin. To the Griffin Judge then, since we are in his land. But where will we *really* go?" Some gods are false; some have limited power; some are powerful among their worshippers but hostile to foreigners. "Silver Bells thinks he will be a snake. Do you suppose he is right?"

"He is always right."

"And you will become a butterfly."

"I never cared much for butterflies," she confessed. "Such frail and helpless creatures. Perhaps I can join you as a snake."

"Oh no. Snakes are for men. Phallic, you see."

"At least I can visit you as a butterfly."

140

"Our guests will cease their chatter and climb the stairs."

We did not feel like guests when they bound our hands and feet to the pole atop the dais. They bound us with leather thongs and, in spite of their gentleness, their obvious effort not to flaw our looks, the ragged fibers cut into our skin.

"Is this the way to treat an honored guest?" asked Marguerite, looking a queen, sounding ready to order an execution.

The Achaeans stared at her as if to say, "How better to serve the God?" and hurried to take their places in the crowd.

Alone with Marguerite, I looked at the Cretans who had come to look at us. Death, torture, shame, or even escape? They could not predict our fate, but they could not fail to be pleased in pleasing their god.

A wall of spiked timbers divided the audience from the arena but did not break their view, since their lowest seats were higher than the spikes. Tier after tier rose upward in soapstone as tall as a three-story house, imprisoning us with multiple rings and the waiting multitudes. The ladies flickered their parasols as if to deflect the sun, but the turn of a wrist, a parasol lowered to hide a face, or raised to reveal, appeared to be part of a courting ritual and what, for the Cretans, must have passed for love. Some wore hats atop their lacquered hair. The young wore open blouses to flaunt their breasts, which were painted in gold, vermilion, purple, or blue to match the voluminous skirts. The men had dressed according to their

141

years: the young and lithe, in phallus sheaths, a ring, and anklet, sandals of ibex leather. What adornment could compete with the truth? The old affected a loose-flowing robe to their knees or ankles, and the color, it seemed, implied their wealth or station: brown for the poor, purple or red for the rich. But while I saw old age, white hair, and wrinkled skin, I looked in vain—except among the poor—for deformities, a limp, a severed limb, a twisted nose. Cretan aristocrats expose the deformed and even the ugly at birth. Any ungainliness is anathema to them.

The clamor remained unbroken until we were bound to the pole: the stare, the conjecture, the awe. The voices were loud since the speakers wished to be heard, and the artfully built arena did not distort the sound; words and phrases reached my ears and did not, must I confess, entirely displease me. For Marguerite, a frequent "Beautiful!" or "Hair like a saffron crocus." For me, "Blonde as the lady, and slim as a Cretan. But half a head taller at least!"

Then, like a canvass lowered to smother a fire, silence muffled the crowd, the silence of expectation. We could only wait with them, but for a different end: to be a surprise instead of to watch a surprise.

In spite of my thongs, I managed to clasp Marguerite by the hand. I felt her tremble—her fingers were slender and small—little-girl hand—and tightened my grip and wished I were Silver Bells to assuage her fear.

"Cousin, Cousin," I said. "We've seen worse times."

"Once," she shuddered. "Since, it was never so bad. Not even among the Tritons." Back to back, we could not face each other, but I envisioned the color leaving her cheeks, and leaving her lovelier: the blue-as-gentian eyes, intensified by her sudden pallor and chill.

"It may not be so bad as we think. We may be part of a festival or a frolic. Have you met any Cretans who look like killers, except the fishermen? They never even make war except against pirates, and then with battering rams instead of hand to hand. They use their spears and axes in rituals, not in combat. Don't confuse them with the Achaeans, who ape them in other ways."

"They are brilliant artists," she said. "Consummate merchants and seamen. They are also children, who will order the death of a slave and go to market without a second thought. They don't look hard or cruel because they feel no guilt. And children like to play. They like their games and their toys. Oryx, we're the toys. Do you understand?"

I had never heard her speak with such despair. Usually she tried to shield me from the truth. Now, it seemed, she felt it best to prepare me for the truth.

The silence, the wait, though probably brief, appeared as endless as watching an hour-glass empty its sands. I tried to fill the time by studying faces until I could see them as individuals and not as a crowd. I recognized wealthy visitors from Egypt, a merchant

143

fat in linen; a dark, purple-lipped soldier whose veins must mingle Egyptian and Libyan blood; a lady as slender as a sapling palm, as graceful and pliant to her companion's words. I saw our host of the villa, protuberant stomach hidden for the occasion. He returned my look with pride; he had found us for the Games and thus he had earned the gratitude of his friends and the blessing of his God. I saw a youth who must have been a prince, Minos' son, no doubt, since he wore a tall, peacock plume in his carefully structured hair and occupied a position close to the ring and shut from the crowd by a makeshift circle of palms. Guards stood behind him; beside him sat a Nubian lady, a queen or at least a princess, attended by pygmies and a plump, laughable fellow who must be a jester of sorts. I had seen such pygmies in Egypt, and jesters with tiger tails affixed to hats and flopping down their backs. But the lady, the princess, the queen, the *Goddess!* A woman to fill your eye, and how she shamed the mantis-waisted Cretans with her amplitudes, her breasts like pumpkins ripe to be plucked, dominating her bold and barbarous gown of tiger skin. A lusty queen of the South! I gave her a tentative smile. Perhaps she would take offence. Perhaps she had learned the ways of a Pharaoh's wife.

She looked at me fixedly, smiled, and gave me an undeniable wink.

Zoe!

"Marguerite," I cried, "Zoe has come to the games. See! Sitting beside the prince among the palms!"

"I see a Nubian queen and attendant pygmies.

Otherwise, there is no resemblance except in girth. This lady's skin is brown, and so is her hair.

"Disguise."

"I see no pointed ears."

"The tips are hidden. They may be forked for all you can see. But they aren't, because they belong to Zoe."

"Oryx, you are snatching at butterflies! How could Zoe be here, and with a Cretan prince, and dressed in such disgusting robe?"

"Disgusting?" I wanted to slap her face! Anger is better than fear at such a time. So is talk. *"It's what men like."* An unfair argument to throw at a woman.

But a rising murmur drowned her reply. A door had opened in the arena floor. A head appeared in the light, eyes blinking, face kindly and sad and also bemused.

"Silver Bells."

He climbed the underground stairs which we could not see and stood in the sun and saw us and smiled. But his smile sent a chill, like a lizard, down my back. I read in his face that he did not know his fate.

And then, another and larger door, and a creature of darkness slouched into the sun.

At first I took her to be a lion. The tawny fur. The tumbling mane and slanted eyes. The enormous padded feet with their deadly claws. No, I saw the black and bristling wings.

"A Sphinx," gasped Marguerite.

"Never mind," I said, grasping for words. They

145

can't really fly, you know. They can only flutter, and
then they fall to the earth."

"How should I *not* know, Oryx? But they don't
really need to fly. There's nothing they need to escape. And some of them can change—"

With a courage I did not feel I met the Sphinx's
stare. "We have seen your kind before," I cried. "And
escaped. And here we are to escape you again. Or kill
you in our attempt."

"Cousin," asked Marguerite, pressing my hand with
desperate strength. "Can it be *her?*"

*A Sphinx who has tracked you never forgets your
scent.*

Chapter Ten

Oryx

The Sphinx entrapped us in her unreadable stare. Composite of Beasts, she had the look of a creating god's mistake: of parts unmatched and at war: wings of a Harpy, mane and paws of a lion but always, and first, the essence of Shark, the unpredictability, the motiveless cruelty. And the essence showed in the eyes. I felt the nameless and indescribable fear of a sailor adrift at sea, land out of sight, when he spies the gliding fin and the lidless eyes. But the eyes of the Sphinx can change their color, reveal instead of conceal. When she is making her kill, they revolve in her head, the gray is speckled with gold, and enigma becomes intention: to maim and torture and kill.

She turned her seeing, unseeing stare to Silver Bells. The shark is a mindless killer; the Sphinx deliberates before she kills; the Sphinx can think. If she wished to feed, Marguerite and I were a waiting feast. But she knew that Silver Bells was our champion. He would protect us. Him she must first destroy.

"You must give him a weapon," I shouted. "How can he fight a Sphinx without even armor? She will tear him to pieces." I thought of the reddish hair

147

which would deepen with blood. I thought of the generous heart which would feel for its friends to its final gallant beat.

I thought of the Sphinx, unconquerable through her shaggy fur, her hide as tough as a warrior's cuirass; conquerable only through her eyes and her mouth. The eyes were small for her size, and shielded in part by her mane. And who could break the barricade of her teeth?

The young Minos rose to his fullest height—most of his royalty, not to mention his height, lay in the peacock plume—and he looked a youth instead of a man: smooth, bland, beardless (the Cretans shave with a blade of bronze); and markedly unintelligent for a race remarkable in their nimble wits as well as their agile feet. Age had settled neither compassion nor hardness on his face, which awaited the chisel of the gods, and doubtless would wait—and resist—and wait until he died. He wore a high, jeweled collar above his naked chest. He jangled with armlets and anklets and doubtless priceless gems—I could only catch the glint of a green, a blue, a purple (amethyst, stone of kings); the glitter of silver and gold.

He assumed the stance which says, "I am going to make a speech, and you, my soon-to-be subjects, shall be my audience—as long as I choose." But a prince is not a king; the eventual Minos XIV was not his resolute father, Minos XIII. The people had come to the games; they met and answered his look: talk as long as you like, you will not be heard. We have come for blood and not for words.

148

The legs of the Sphinx were bound by ropes whose nethermost ends were fixed to invisible bars beneath the ground, but the animal fretted; the ropes had begun to fray. And the crowd was fretful for games.

"In honor of Him, the God, to whom the bull is the holiest of the animals, we have organized these Games. The God has sent us an earthly surrogate; a Bull-man from the northern forests of Crete. He is pitted against a Sphinx, anathema to the God, his Mother, and men who worship them." The Prince was speaking what his people knew; they could *see* the contestants; they wanted to see them fight. Rumbles, like the warning snorts of the Bull who holds the island atop his back, before he topples a wall or crumbles a palace with his weapons of soil and stone, ran through the crowd, met, swelled, threatened a quake of men instead of earth. "If the Minotaur wins the fight, our vineyards will flourish with grapes. If he loses, the omens are bad." The Prince, sensing the restlessness in his subjects, looked to Zoe for praise, encouragement, words to continue his speech. Quickly she shook her head. The Prince completed his speech in a single breath.

"Butthatisthewayofthegames. Thuswelearnthewill-oftheGod."

"Let 'em fight. Crops 'ull take care o' themselves!"

The nameless speaker appeared to speak for the crowd.

"Fight to the death!"

After my scrutiny, they had seemed to revert into a shapeless whole. Like a monster jelly fish, they un-

149

dulated over the seats and moved of a single accord; with a few exceptions, I guessed, they wished with a single horrendous wish.

"They don't care at all who wins," sighed Marguerite. "They don't want to please their God. They just want to see some blood. Hide their heartlessness under the name of ritual."

Perhaps, in earlier ages, when Woman instead of Man had ruled on Crete, such games had been a genuine ritual; no more. Marguerite was right. Bigger ships and smaller hearts; thus, the Cretans of now.

"It's enough to make me turn to thieving again. That is to say, if Zoe hadn't reformed me. I could spend a lifetime robbing these folk."

"Hush," said Marguerite. You tempt whatever demons may be in this place. You speak of a lifetime. Better to speak of a moment, or nothing at all."

"Throw him a weapon!" we shouted in one great voice. They had probably not even bothered to learn his name; to them, he was a Beast, and a Beast was less than Human, however dear to their God. A griffin was meant for a pet; a dolphin for food; a bull or Bull-man for sacrifice.

No one had heard us above the crowd. Suppose he had heard the pleas of his prisoners: The Prince would have done as he chose or sought the advice of courtiers and counselors. But even a simpleton must foresee that a weaponless Silver Bells might die at the first confrontation, and an early death would lessen the sport. Still, he made no move till Zoe whispered

into his royal ear. The Prince removed the dagger from his side—small, bronze of hilt and onyx of blade, I assumed—and threw it into the ring. His gesture was grand; he paused and posed and waited in vain for acclaim. "And throw him a flagon of wine. The day is hot. We would have him fight at his best."

Silver Bells, retrieving the dagger, leaving the wine on the ground, turned to the dais and Marguerite and me. "I am the forest," he said. "You are the city. But the two have met as friends. Will you bless my weapon against our enemy?"

"Silver Bells! It is you I will bless," cried Marguerite. "You fight with more than a dagger, you fight with my love."

"I give you my heart," he said. "It is all I have." He spoke to both of us, and I knew that he loved us as friends. But she thought his avowal was meant for her; she understood "love" to mean "desire."

Such was our parting. Well, I was glad. Alyssum's ghost was a rival she could not match. But if he should die, she would think herself first at the last, and her grief for him would be strangely sweet.

The ropes had been loosed from the Sphinx's feet, and she crouched above the door, which was barred and effaced into the dirt of the ring. She did not advance on her foe; she did not circle to spy his weaknesses. She flaunted the pride of her strength. (But then to a Sphinx, a Nubian lion is weak.)

Silver Bells did not wait for her to move; waiting was not his way, when his friends were bound to a pole. With the speed of my namesake, the oryx, he crossed the ring and kicked her with his hoof. The hoof of a Minotaur is harder than that of a bull. He ought to have smashed her face. But her face is thick with fur and armored with cartilage.

She recoiled with mild surprise. A Sphinx does not feel pain, but droplets of blood bespattered the sand. The eyes remained impassive and gray.

And then she moved, and the movement belonged to a lion.

"He is gone," said Marguerite, in a flat, emotionless voice, as if she had said, "He is dead."

"Gone? Why, he stands—"

He did not stand.

"He has drowned in a yellow sea," she said.

The Sphinx had squatted atop his body and shut him from the air. (Surely the Harpies had lent her those fluttering wings but forgotten to give them flight.)

"She is smothering him to death," I gasped. "Not even a hand or foot is left in view!"

She sat with equanimity upon her prey. He did not appear to struggle under her weight. He appeared to lack the means.

An incongruous image, all the more horrible for its incongruity, flickered into my mind: a giant hen sitting on her egg. If she looked like many animals, a sphinx played as many parts, bland, guileful, ludicrous, but always returned to the cruelty of a shark. She knew that horror without relief eventually dulls. Thus, she changed her guise—with suggestion, illu-

sion, (physical change?), to stir the deadening and
renew the fear.

It was the yellow eyes which denied the hen and
reasserted the shark . . . staring at Marguerite . . .
staring at me. I think that she tried to smile. A shark's
downturned mouth is curved perpetually to the re-
verse of a smile; it is curved to swallow or rend. And
yet . . . and yet . . .

"Oryx, jerk on your thongs, you have got to get us
free!"

"I've jerked until my wrists are open wounds.
Ankles too."

"So are mine. And the pole won't bend."

I could not see her face, bound as we were to opposite sides of a pole; but I could guess her look. The
alabaster features were cracked with grief; a sob was
lodged in her throat.

"Do you think he is dead?" she choked. She
wanted a shouted "No!"

Yes, I thought, he is dead, and I loved him above
all men. I loved his strength and his courage; I loved
the silken mane and the rock-hard hooves. I wanted
to be a Beast like him. *I loved him for loving without judging, except the wantonly cruel.*

But the heart, like a pyramid, has many rooms and
they were flooded with grief for Silver Bells; but more
for Marguerite, who was mother, sister, and friend to
me. That I should die—well, I had grown accustomed
to change, and I must confess to a curiosity about the
Afterlife (I have told you my liking for snakes). But
not Marguerite; her lotus-skin, her gentian-eyes, her

crocus-yellow hair in the maw of a being which even the God, when a cruel and prankish boy, could never have twisted into the light. . . . life in the maw of death.

Silver Bells she had smothered; us she will tease and torture, like a griffin teasing a nightingale, for we are no possible threat to her; she will tear off a limb, toss, shake, grind us into the dirt. The world has tilted atop the turtle's back, and evil encompasses us like the inky juice of the squid.

She rose to her haunches. The movement was not precipitate. In her slow, deliberate way she was coming for us.

Behind her she left the body of Silver Bells. The bells were stripped from his horns and mangled in the dust. Nausea rose in my throat like that furry spider, the Jumper, with knotted legs.

Behind her she left a trickle of blood.

Somehow, under that crushing weight, that smothering fur, he had driven his knife through the fur and into her underbelly. Oh, he had hardly struck her a mortal blow. He had merely pierced the skin and perhaps the cartilage. But he had angered her. She paused and turned and stared at the impudent creature who ought to be dead.

The pale red chest expanded with air.

He lives, he lives. . . . Silver Bells, where is your knife?

He seemed to have lost his will. She raised a leisurely paw and talons projected like the quills on the back of a Libyan porcupine. He could not even roll from her path.

But the paw remained in the air, as if transfixed by an invisible rope. Something had joined blood-lust in her face. Surprise.

She shrugged, as if to dislodge a noxious mosquito; she lashed her tail in annoyance. She stared at the dais, at Marguerite and me. Were we the cause of her aggravation? Impossible.

One of her lidless eyes revolved in its socket, yellow fading to gray, gray bespeckled with blood.

"Someone has injured an eye," I cried.

"But who—"

"Zoe!"

"No. Zoe's pygmies, at her command. The Goat Girls. That's why she brought them with her. No one is looking at them. See. There! The slings. Hidden under their robes. They fire a pebble and quickly hide the sling. Have you ever seen such speed? And Silver Bells is starting to move!"

Not dead, not dead. . . . Oh, to raise my arms and shout a prayer to the sky or kneel and hug the earth! To wreath an altar or garland an image with laurel and hyacinths!

Silver Bells brushed the ground in search of the knife; perhaps it was caught in the Sphinx's fur. He found the flagon of wine.

"Is he going to drink?"

"He must be dazed. He thinks he has found the knife."

Holding the flagon, he crouched and lowered his

head; attacking, the Sphinx would meet his horns.
Perhaps they would wound her but scarcely more
than the knife.

She circled him warily; at least he had taught her
caution.

"Can he get the other eye?"

"With what? A flagon of wine?"

She paused above him and slowly lowered her
bulk. His horns were caught in her mane. She knew
that he had not found the knife.

"Suffocation again."

Silver Bells' movements seemed both sluggish and
dazed. His hand was uselessly slow, or so it seemed to
me; perhaps it was only slow when compared to my
wing-heeled wish!

"She can't close her jaws. He's wedged the flagon
between them!"

"But this time he's truly dead. He has closed his
eyes."

The death of hope in a friend is the bite of a thousand ants.

"No!" I shouted. "Silver Bells is immortal."

"Even the gods may die. Who can withstand a
Sphinx?"

And then she came for us.

She came, she came,
inevitable as the tide (under what moon's
    compulsion?),
but not the friendly touching of the sea . . .
Riptide, Triton-tide,

To steal, rend, kill . . .
Slowly. . . . .
The beach is entrapped by the earth and has no
weapon against the sea.

Egypt . . . the lotus pool . . . the remembered
scent. She had followed us all of these years and
found us on Crete.

"I wish she had killed us then," said Marguerite.
The ghost of a child, she seemed, bodiless on the
wind. Thin, far words . . . sad, sad, like prickles
of frost in the face. "We were meant to die. We must
have angered a god."

"No! The years we have had were good."

"But we have killed Silver Bells. Except for
us. . . ."

The stairs ascended directly in front of me, and
only I could watch her ascent. Paw over deadly paw,
she climbed the stairs; she seemed to drag, but not
from her wound. I think she wished to delay and
heighten the feast. She could not dislodge the flagon
and shut her jaws; she could not truly smile. And yet
I saw delight in her single, seeing eye; gray, it glittered with yellow flecks.

The shaggy fur, how loathsome it must have become in the dirt of the ring: There should be a scent
of blood. But the fur looked immaculate, the blood
invisible, and the scent was curiously that of a melon,
one of those oval fruits with succulent yellow centers
from the Nile. Shark-like in eyes, cat-like in cleanli-

ness. *She will feast and lick her paws until she is clean.*

I felt the heat of her body and shrank against the pole. A leather-tough paw, claws retracted into their sheaths, pressed me lightly against the arm. I waited until the paw should project its claws; recoiled against the post (and wished it into a spear).

Fear has been called a spider in the throat or a lizard along the spine. Such are little fears. Fear at its worst is reversal: night instead of day, order disordered, creation uncreated. It is being alone in an infinite dark. Neither sun nor moon nor companionable stars . . . neither sound of voices nor scent of grass and trees . . . neither Marguerite nor Zoe nor Silver Bells nor even those bad little Goat Girls with their unerring slings.

Thus do the pharaohs companion their mummies with what they have loved on the earth, the sceptres and pectorals, the boats and the chariots . . . even the slaves (once, it is said, the wives and the children, the friends and the concubines—except for the eldest son and heir to the throne).

I was afraid of the dark.

She enclosed my shoulder within her mouth. I felt the tongue like a brush, a bristle with hairs from a hog. I felt the teeth like a row of broken knives.

The jaws began to close. . . .

She did not make a sound. In all of that time, she did not make a sound. A Triton hisses, a Harpy shrills . . . Not her, not the Sphinx.

159

Till now.

A single cry, and I thought she would burst my ears. A wind devil's shriek; the thunder which follows the jagged spear of the God. Sounds which were sucked from a stormy sky, from the God's domain (though even he had disavowed the Sphinx).

She had forgotten the flagon between her jaws.

The waterless desert is the home of a Sphinx. A Sphinx is afraid of water. Wine is the watery juice of the grape.

The odor of rotting melon was rank in the air.

The crowd, hushed with the splendid drama of their Games, the gore, the death of the Sphinx, emitted a universal shriek of exultation. Not that it mattered to them who had died. They would sooner have cheered the Sphinx, I suspect, for she would have teased and devoured us and extended the Games. Still, their Bull-man had won, and against unthinkable odds, with surprises, reversals, and blood.

Only then did they see to Silver Bells. Achaeans opened the doors in the pit, entered the ring, and lifted him to his feet. He did not greet the Prince; he looked at me; he looked at Marguerite.

I whispered a "thank you, Silver Bells" and saw from his smile that he could read my lips. Marguerite had dissolved into noisy tears.

"Cousin," I teased, feeling a little drunk, "you have forgotten your trade. Courtesans *never* bawl." I squeezed her hand and called to the guards for our release. The guards awaited an order from the Prince.

Minos rose to his feet and raised a wobbling spear. (He ought to have watched Eunostos to learn the art.) The cheers became sporadic, faded, and died into expectation. They turned to their prince, these curious people, to learn his plans for us. We had come as captives into the ring. We had surely earned our freedom, but Cretans negotiate in curious currency.

"The God has spoken through his mortal exemplar. The Bull-man has killed the Sphinx!"

The words rang clearly across the ring and up and down the tiers. He was going to make a speech.

"Set him free?" he echoed, looking about him to see who presumed to demand. "But he was never our prisoner. He was our honored guest!"

"But you kept him in shackles and risked his life." Zoe, reminding but not reproachful.

The young man shook his head in befuddlement. She leaned to his ear and whispered inaudible words.

"Silver Bells," he commanded. "Approach us and receive your reward."

Silver Bells shrugged the Achaeans away from him. With infinite dignity and yet with a limp which made him infinitely touching, woundingly lovable, he approached the Prince in his circle of palms. He did not bow or kneel.

"And let him bring his friends!" Zoe, still in command of the Prince's ear.

Thomas Burnett Swann

"Untie them, untie them. But I have *not* decided—"

And thus we stood before the Prince and Zoe and the miraculous Goat Girls, and the jester, Phlebas, swinging the tiger tail around his head; and of course Eunostos, the King of the Pygmies. His hat, awry, revealed a pointed ear. I made him a secret sign and he hid the ear. (Did I hear a muffled "Cor" from one of the Girls?)

"Silver Bells, we would like you to join the Court and—"

"Become a curiosity," he said. "I want to return to the Country."

"Return to the Country," echoed Phlebas. "And keep my tail for proof. That I have had an Adventure!"

"The King of the Pygmies and I will sail them there in the *Nilus*," announced Zoe, a wonder of womanhood to dazzle a princelier prince, "before I return to Nubia to honor our trade agreement with Crete."

"And we'll go too," I shouted, clasping my cousin's hand. "Won't we, Eun—uh, your Littleness."

Eunostos looked to the Prince. "The Bull-man has surely earned the freedom of your other guests. I request that they be permitted to join Queen Zoe and me on our ship and return to Nubia with us." His voice was manly and strong for a child of eight.

The Prince was slow to answer; an intimation of thought appeared in his face. A reservation. He was, I fear, an excessively dense young man. He liked to

162

be told while seeming to give commands; at the same time, he wanted to please the people whom he was destined to rule. Marguerite and I—well, we were not indispensable to the Cretans, in spite of her beauty and our golden hair. They could free us and feel no irreparable loss. But a Minotaur who could duel with a Sphinx and win! What other court could boast such a wonderment?

"Remember our agreement," Zoe reminded, smiling her most irresistible smile (her least irresistible smile is hard to resist). "Slaves from my sturdiest tribes."

Perplexity from the Prince.

"Ivory."

Indecision.

"Apes."

A look at his people to gauge their wish. Uncertainty trembling on the verge of a "now." (Perhaps I could steal an armlet—the amethyst? His stubbornness gave me license to resume my trade.)

"Last night."

A beatific smile illumined his face.

"Last night," he murmured, rising to order his guards. "The Queen of Nubia and the King of the Pygmies shall have their wish." Authority ruled the indecisive voice.

Zoe winked at me. The time away from her tree had sapped her strength but neither her spirit nor looks. "I have always had a way with younger men, eh, Oryx?"

Chapter Eleven

Zoe

The *Nilus*, low in the water, eased a sluggish course toward the northern forest, the beach of embarkation, the Country of the Beasts. The sail, straining with wind to pull its passengers, looked like a Cyclops' puffed and swollen cheek. The Goat Girls plied the oars without complaint and Melissa, proud though garlandless, stood at the till and alternated her look between the horizon and her hero, Oryx. We were dangerously crowded since Silver Bells, Oryx, and Marguerite had joined the crew. But who could worry at such a triumphant time? The Prince had sent a pair of galleys as escorts—long and sleek and painted with purple moons—sea gull on the prow in cedarwood; marlin's tail at the stern—for fear some roving Tritons should sink us and capture us, and make another sale, to a master of games in another town. (If I were disclosed as a Dryad, what would they pay for me, in the prime of my years with my green-as-a-maple-leaf hair, its gray discreetly concealed by a twist of curls? I would doubtless fetch as much as a Minotaur—that is to say, except for Silver Bells.)

"Zoe," said Silver Bells. "You are a queen in truth. You have done the work of a queen and I, your subject, salute you as I may." He dipped his horns; and his bells, which I had laboriously straightened and reattached to his horns, reverberated an argent melody. I read in his words an unaccustomed warmth, or did my wishes exceed the truth? Alyssum, eternal Alyssum, *she* had never delivered her man from a Sphinx. I loved her; truly I loved the blue-haired Naiad, with her sweet and obstinate ways. But a rival, even though dead, especially when dead because she remains perfected in the heart, arouses fear as well as love, at least in the imperfection known as Zoe, Dryad of Crete.

"The umber is starting to run," I smiled. "My tiger skin robe is making me want to scratch. Is scratching a royal gesture? I hardly have strength to stand. And I am a queen?" I waited hopefully for a heated denial (even a gallant lie).

Phlebas—may Hermes press his olive-sized brain!— hurried to interrupt.

"But the Sphinx. Where did they get her, Zoe? I thought they were gone from Crete." Adventure had heightened his fancy and also increased his size. He had dined with the Prince and eaten a squid, a pheasant, a parrot fish, and a suckling pig. He did not look like an adolescent goat; trim the fur and behold, a walking feast!

"They are. The Minotaurs drove them into the

sea—oh, toward the end of the Silver Age. They can't swim a stroke, you know—the water poisons them—and the Tritons ate their remains."

"And most of the Minotaurs died in the fight," said Silver Bells. "There were ten of us for every one of them, but you have seen how they fight. That's why Eunostos and I are the last of our race. That and the wolves."

I shook a tear from my eye with a rapid turn of my head. "But of course a Sphinx can become a beautiful woman. Or so it is whispered by the country folk. And then she is called a Lamia. No one has ever seen the change. Still, it is thought to happen from the deeds of the women. Nefarious. For that matter, who can see a windstorm, and yet we can guess her presence when the trees bend down their boughs—and sometimes break."

"What was that word you said, Aunt Zoe?"

"Nefarious."

"Liking affairs, you mean?"

"Wicked. Such changeable creatures are frequent in every land. Zeus can become a snake or a bull. Proteus changes to suit his whim."

"Are any Lamias left on Crete?"

"Not that I know. They generally keep to desert lands. Egypt. Lybia. The Cretans told me that this particular Sphinx assumed the guise of a Lamia, sailed to Phaistos without arousing suspicion, and then reverted to Sphinx. You see, with their love for ugliness, they do not like to remain for long as women. They will only change to work their evil designs. To move without detection and prey on children at night or break the hearts of men and drink their blood. They prefer to look—well, like an afterthought of a god whose name we do not remember. One of the old Sumerian gods, perhaps, forgotten with his decaying kingdom."

"I think she came for *us*," said Oryx. "Marguerite and me. She has probably tracked us since we were children." Quickly he told me about the death of his parents and how he and Marguerite had escaped and fled and dreaded a Sphinx which might have caught their scent. It was not an easy confession. He looked like a man instead of the callow youth who had grabbed me behind the oak; I could swear he had grown since he came to the Country; muscles beneath the sun-saffroned skin; slender waist but broadening shoulders. Still, he had to return for the moment to little boy, the fear and the flight. His eyes grew dim with remembering and blue retreated to gray; his husky voice descended into a gasp. I placed a hand on his arm and reproached myself for reproaching his thievery.

"But how could that creature know we would come to Phaistos?" asked Marguerite. Practical girl... except when she looked at Silver Bells.

"Harpies," I said. "The Harpies are friends of the Sphinxes. Allies in evil. Both of them winged and ugly and bent on destruction. You have already told me how the Harpies attacked your ship on your way to Crete. They saw you again in the Country of the Beasts—they circle our skies, you see—but may not

167

have known of your ancient quarrel with their friends. But a Harpy can fly to Libya in a single day. One of them flew, it would seem, and told the Sphinxes of spotting you in the Country, and the Sphinx who remembered your scent proceeded to make her plans. She took the form of a woman and sailed to Crete—a rapid trip in midsummer—and waited for further news. The Harpies alerted her when you left the Country—together with Silver Bells—and Tritons captured your boat and sold you for the Games. She assumed her rightful shape, allowed herself to be caught, and met you in the ring. To get at the two of you, she must first kill Silver Bells. Not that she minded, you understand. Indeed, she seemed to exult at the chance. Perhaps she remembered the old ancestral feud."

"And the scent of Oryx and me," shuddered Marguerite, a monument to disordered loveliness. "And how we hid in the pool and she tracked us these many years."

I liked her; Zoe, I said in my thoughts, you like Marguerite. The Country has cured her of her affected ways (and probably ruined the skills of her trade). I wanted to hate her because of Silver Bells; she loved him, of that I was sure. But when has Zoe lost to a human rival (even with golden hair)?

"Are we truly saved?" asked Oryx. "We saw her escape from the ring as a butterfly."

"What you saw was her soul."

"Can a soul revert to the shape of a Sphinx?"

"No," I said. "A butterfly she remains. She can

harm you no more than an actual butterfly, buffeted by the rains or chased by birds. A soul is immortal, of course, whether good or bad. But if you can catch her, you can destroy her incarnation and she will wander forever without a house, prey to the winds and, like them, invisible. Yes, you are safe. Now I must rest. How many days from my tree? Five or six, I should think. Well, I am strong. I was longer away with my Babylonian lover, though he had his little tricks to lessen the pain. But someone else will have to captain the ship, and it can't be Silver Bells. For he needs a rest like me, what with being a couch for a Sphinx and feeling the gash of her claws. Phlebas, fan me, will you, my dear? You may use your tail."

"Isn't it rather short?"

"The tiger's tail, not your own. Now then, who will be captain?"

"I" said Eunostos.

"I'm older," said Oryx. "The duty should fall to me."

"Yes," said Melissa, "the duty should fall to Oryx."

"But I was taught by my uncle." Polite but firm. "Besides, these are Triton waters, and you're a foreigner, Oryx."

"Eunostos is captain," I said.

"You there, Bindweed, throw me a line."

Bindweed obeyed without a "cor."

I had never known a Beastlier boy. His hooves were sharp; he had learned dexterity, not display, with his tail; and his straight-feathered cap disclosed his

169

pointed ears. But then with Silver Bells for an uncle. . . .

"And I will look after Silver Bells," said Marguerite, sweetly solicitous (sincere, I could not doubt, but comelier than I chose, and not like me athirst for her father tree).

"Silver Bells," I asked. "You are very quiet. Do your injuries pain you much?" His chest was a map of scratches; his bones must ache from his fight. He had chipped a hoof and lost considerable blood. In a phrase, he hurt.

"Less than your need for your tree. Sweet dreams, Zoe."

"And to you," I said. *Of* you, I wanted to say. I merely smiled. I have never been one to chase a man. (I have never needed to chase.)

"Land ahoy!"

I lifted my head. The effort cost me hurt. Weariness like a chain affixed me to the couch. But the land was the beach in the cove from which both the cockleshell and the *Nilus* had begun their voyages. I smelled the cyclamen trailing from the cliffs. I counted the cypresses and Melissa looked for violets. I numbered the boats on the beach. I thought of my father tree. "Daughter," he seemed to say. "Rest from your journey in my leafy arms. Return to child. Forget, remember, renew." A dream, a dream. Part of my weakening, like a vision which comes with a demon of fever or plague.

Nevertheless, the beach was real.

The two Cretan captains, seeing us safe from Tritons and ready to land, reversed their courses and made for the East and home. I lifted a heavy hand. One of the captains bowed and the other winked—I believe I had filled their eye, woman as well as queen. Splendid men, the seamen of Crete, and not like the city-folk. The old yearning lingers in their blood. They have sailed beyond the Pillars of Hercules. They have crossed Oceanus to a land so large that they could not find its end, though they landed and traded with men who wore feathers and painted their beardless cheeks. To search is more than to find. To find is more than to keep. . . . So far as they knew, we would disembark Silver Bells, Oryx, and Marguerite and, thus relieved of excessive weight and safe from a Triton attack, sail for the Nile and, partly by caravan because of the cataracts, return to Nubia. I did not like to deceive such men. In an earlier time, we might have been friends and allies.

Moschus pranced excitedly onto the beach. He had spied us from the cliffs; he must have kept a vigil for our return. Faithful friend! I earnestly hoped that beer had eased his wait (he had a cache in the hull of a rotting boat). Eunostos and Phlebas sprang from the deck and, splattering foam, joined Moschus to beach the ship. Bindweed and Hensbane lifted me from the couch.

"Mind my robe," I said. "Don't soil the stripes." It was the only time I had been a queen. It saddened me to forego the perquisites of power. A Dryad rules a tree, at most an Asklepion. But *I* had dined with the

Prince who was heir to the throne of Crete; The other four Girls—I could never remember their names—jumped from the ship and caught me in surprisingly gentle arms and settled me on the beach. They must have bathed in seawater during the trip; they did not smell of goat.

"See?" cried Moschus. "I have brought a bough from your father tree. And a skin of beer from my own private store."

I grasped the bough and smothered my face in its reviving leaves. Only a tree can heal, but a bough can act as balm, and it gave me the strength to stand, supported by Moschus and a generous swig of beer, and I turned to confront my friends.

"I am very proud," I said.

"Why, Aunt Zoe?" Eunostos asked, shaking the seawater from his hooves.

"Because of my faithful friends. Do you realize what you have done?"

"You, not us," he corrected. "You were our queen and you planned our triumph and saved my uncle from death. Did you really expect us to fail?"

"So much wickedness stood in our way!"

"And you trampled it under foot."

"At times I had my doubts."

"But you hid them from us and never lost your smile!"

"Noblesse oblige," I muttered.

"Are you speaking Sumerian?" Phlebas asked. "Learned from that lover you mentioned?"

"Babylonian, *not* Sumerian. Do you take me for a crone? Now then. Everyone to his house."

Melissa lived in a hollow log, a garland of daisies over the door. Silver Bells and Eunostos had built a workshop under the ground and planted their roof with carrots and radishes. The Goat Girls moved from cave to cave and called the forest their home. Phlebas, like Moschus, enjoyed the hospitality of his friends.

To reach my father tree, I had to lean on Moschus, not the steadiest Centaur on four hooves. Once I recover my strength, I thought, I shall lean on no one but Silver Bells, and *he* shall rescue *me* instead of Alyssum or Marguerite. Once I recover my strength. . . .

"Moschus," I said, averting my lips from his intended kiss (his kisses were always wet and lingering. I always felt as if beer had been sloshed in my face. At certain times in the past, I had suffered the slosh. Now I had expectations.) "Did you miss me, my dear?"

"The Country was like a nest without an egg," he said, preening himself on the doubtful compliment (I had to recall that he liked an egg in his beer). "In fact, your absence has driven me to drink. I think you should give an orgy to celebrate."

My previous orgy could not be called a success. As a hostess, perhaps I am too unsettling to be at my best; an ideal hostess effaces herself in the crowd; looks to her guests, their pleasure, their food and drink. Alas, in spite of myself, I invariably overshadow my entertainment, my choicest dish, my oldest wine, and end as dessert.

"Orgies must wait," I said.

"Until you've regained your strength," said Silver Bells. "Then I will ask the Naiads to entertain you under one of their springs. You won't have to do a thing."

The Naiads are blue-haired ladies whose caverns under the water are treasure troves of the gems they collect in the springs: Shy, gentle ladies—except Alyssum, stubborn as well as kind—and no more obtrusive than a cooling breeze.

Since Alyssum's death, Silver Bells had avoided Alyssum's people. Why the change? Of course! An engagement party! Having at last recovered from his grief, he wished to make his announcement among her kin, a courtesy as it were, to tell them that he had never intended to exclude them from his affairs; accept their forgiveness for the apathy of his grief.

"Give me a week," I said. "Then you will see the Zoe who captured the heart of the Prince of Crete!"

"Are we invited?" the Goat Girls asked with their usual unanimity. They were seldom invited to parties in the Country. They behaved at their worst, tippled and swore and tried to tease the men with charms which would never bud, much less bloom. But after their faithful attendance in the arena, after their service aboard the ship, how could Silver Bells strike them from his list?

"What is a party without my friends?" asked Silver Bells.

" 'Ear that?" asked Hensbane to Bindweed. "What'll we wear?"

"Nothin'."

"Better ask Zoe, eh? *She* knows the proper weeds."

"Something capacious," I said.

"Think she said a cape. . . ."

"And me? Phlebas asked. "Shall I wear my tiger's tail?"

"What else? It becomes you as if you had grown it yourself."

"I thought as much."

"And I shall string a necklace with violets," Melissa said. And Oryx can escort me from my log."

"But Marguerite and I are still under sentence of exile," reminded Oryx.

"A Naiad party should even soften Chiron. The ladies are famous for their persuasiveness, and Moschus will ply his cousin with drink and loosen his tongue. That is to say, you naughty boy, if you restrain your animalistic desires. We can't have another incident."

He sighed and smiled (the rogue), and I could guess his lecherous thought. "Oh, very well. I shall have to get drunk and avoid temptation."

"Wine increases desire." (Echoes of Chiron.)

"And limits performance. Dead drunk, I mean. I shall probably be carried out with the first course."

A delicate shadow flickered across the ground. A saffron butterfly.

Alyssum perhaps to greet our return?

I could swear she had flown from our ship.

Chapter Twelve

Zoe

When the Centaurs had brought the Naiads from the Orient, they had left a few in Egypt (heavy with colt), and settled the rest on Crete in a fountain home. The Cretan Mother's sister, she of the East (though many say that she and the Mother are One), is said to have spun them along with pigeon-blood rubies and tiger lilies—useless but decorative. They did not weave, they neither gardened nor cleaned the hearth; they danced and sang or played a lyre which they called a "mandolin" and recited poems; took a morning to arrange a flower. To them an hourglass was useless as well as ugly.

Silver Bells had supplied the food; Moschus had brought the wine and the beer (cadged from his friends). Otherwise, we would dine on bird's nest soup.

"And we shall supply the tea and the song," said Thyme, their queen. "For Silver Bells is our friend, and he has returned to us."

I have fallen asleep at their parties, and not from

the tea, which reminds me of muddy water in a porcelain cup.

But tonight, tonight . . . In the ear of my mind I heard my beloved announce,

"Zoe and I shall be wed. I have lived too long with a ghost."

Intoxicated with expectation, what did I need with wine?

Moschus had pleaded to escort me to the cave ("Before I have had a nip!"). Oryx had said, "But we are friends of the road. Why not come with me? (I promise not to pounce)."

"I have an escort," I said (mysterious Zoe, relishing mystery! Let them conjecture who had won my heart. What would they think of a husband instead of a lover?) I went to the party companioned only by hope. I felt like more than a queen; I felt like a girl.

We talk about butterflies in the stomach when we are fearful of danger or ecstatic with hope. The feeling is more like sparrows building a nest! The Naiads would probably mistake me for a mute: talkative Zoe, a griffin has her tongue! Still, I was coming to listen, not to speak, and the words I expected to hear would resound through my head like silver bells (can you think of a better analogy for the occasion?).

I walked the avenue called the Path of the Moon: sand and milky seashells under the stars. Shower-of-gold, Bird-of-paradise, looking as if it could fly, and tamarisk made a western East of the place. I approached the entrance to the Naiad cave, the House

177

of the Seventh Bliss. The ladies, of course, who spend their days in the fountain above their cave, have an entrance under the water, but they do like evening guests, they do like to please, and Silver Bells had dug them a tunnel opening into the forest for those who do not wish or know how to swim.

Two wooden dragons flanked the door. By "dragon" I mean the amiable Eastern kind, more of a watch dog and pet than a brute, bringer of luck and guardian of the cave. The cypress gates were open like welcoming arms, since the Country is free of Sphinxes and wolves; and Satyrs and Centaurs, even if drunk, would never crash a party for Silver Bells. I rang a golden bell in the shape of a bird; its clapper looked like a tongue in a sunbird's mouth.

With short, shuffling steps, one of the Naiads appeared in the door. Marjoram she was called. She wore a loose-fitting robe, caught at her waist with a wide, crimson sash, and reaching to feet so small that they scarcely seemed to fill her embroidered shoes. It was not yet dark; I could see her hair, dried from her swim and cloudy about her head. Not disheveled, you understand. I surmised the careful tease of a tortoiseshell comb. And of course her hair was blue and her eyes were violet. Her skin was as white as the foam from the fountain's tree. You might have thought that the vivid hair and eyes, in contrast to the skin, would have made her look like a woman possessed by a fever or robbed of blood by a Strige's insatiable tongue. Pallid and drained of life. No, she was like an ivory figurine, new and not yet yellowed by the years, with daintily painted features and the hush of an artifact. A work of art, not life. None of the Naiads except Alyssum had looked entirely real. But then, the Eastern Mother had meant them to decorate, and though I preferred an earthier race, I could not quarrel with a goddess' handiwork.

She extended her arms; her voluminous sleeves, as violet as her eyes, fell to her waist. She bowed and smiled a small but immaculate smile; a Naiad never laughs, and every movement, every gesture, is slow, studied, and graceful.

"My house is honored," she said, "most esteemed of my guests, Zoe, the Dryad of Crete. Famed for her travels, envied for her loves, celebrated for beauty these four hundred years. . . ."

"Marjoram, dear," I said. "You may skip the formalities and take me to your guests. By the way, the number is *three*, not four. Hundred, that is."

"Yes, my estimable friend. But age is accounted a virtue in the East."

"In the West, it is gray hairs and a thickening waist. Am I your first guest?"

"The first and the best."

"Then I will chat with you and your friends till the others arrive." I stooped and entered the tunnel and pitied Moschus, who would scrape the walls with his flanks, and rose in the midst of a garden.

Of sorts.

Rocks instead of flowers. Black, contorted plants instead of bushes or trees. Nothing of color, little of

179

life to catch the eye. (But I remembered Bumpers, the Hill. Perhaps I stood on a god.)

Marjoram paused for me to admire the place. "I have seen it before. Lovely," I said, and, never liking to lie, hurried ahead of my hostess into a bare, circular room where the Naiads awaited their guests. "Tea house," they call the place, after their favorite beverage (aptly too), and I hurried to greet my other hostesses before I should have to repeat the lie.

There were ten of them. They did not resemble each other in spite of identical hair and eyes. They wore such a richness of colors—gowns, sleeves, sashes, and slippers—so as to seem a scatter of precious stones. Aquamarine stood next to amethyst, jade to cornelian . . . lapis lazuli, onyx, and peridot. . . . In my mind, I compared them to gems in spite of their flower-like names, for again they were more of art than of life. They shuffled about the room on tiny feet, took my sandals, arranged a cloak around my shoulders (the fountain chilled the room), and seated me on a floor of fitted cypress squares. Yes, on the floor. True, they gave me a mat but the cypress was very hard and the mat of rushes was hardly a chair or a couch. I tried to cross my legs like my hostess and look at ease; I fear I had the look of having stumbled and tried in vain to rise. My feet were crooked, I burst a grasshopper pendant from my gown, and the ache in my rear made me stifle a groan.

The room was unfurnished except for a table with fig-sized cups—much too small for wine—and a plump, snouted vessel called a "pitcher." Unfur-

nished, I say, but I will have to count a "bonsai tree,"
a sort of vegetable dwarf whose limbs are deliberately
stunted like a Naiad's feet, set on a table against the
wall and lit by a lantern hanging from the roof. There
were also mats for the other guests and, hidden behind
a screen enwrought with rock crystal and black jade,
skins of beer from Moschus' depredations, and melons
from Silver Bells' garden, and pheasants, and. . .yes,
Eunostos' choicest carrots.

Well, I had undergone other Naiad parties, without any beer or food and without any expectation.
Only tea, brewed from the camomile plant. ("Tea and
sympathy," Moschus called such parties. "Sympathy
for the guests who must drink the tea.")

The guests arrived in a beautifully awkward group,
chatting excitedly, greeting Thyme and her Naiads
and lifting me from the floor for a hug or a kiss (and
a curious look, as if to ask the name of my new-
est love): Bindweed and Hensbane and their friends
of our voyage, prodigal with their "cor's"; Eunostos
and Silver Bells, arm in arm and smiling at me as if I
belonged between them; Phlebas, stupefied into silence by the exalted occasion (or the seeming lack of
food?). Moschus and Chiron—the Whinnies had
stayed at the gate—both of them wearing jerkins—
Chiron in red with stripes of brown to match his
tufted mane, his unadorned back ashine and scented
with nard; his six wives, no doubt, had spent the
afternoon to groom him for the affair. Melissa, last
of the group, like the nub of a tail which brings up
the rear of a bear.

181

"My sweet," said Chiron to Thyme. "You and your friends have done yourselves proud. But where is the beer? My cousin and I have a thirst."

"First the tea," said Thyme, with the hint of a bow, "and a welcoming song." While her sisters poured the tea, she accompanied herself on a mandolin.

"Tea and sympathy," Chiron muttered

The Fountain Goddess

Under the fountain's liquid tree
A goddess lies asleep
Where Naiads scatter bergamot,
And when the waters leap

With rainbows, yellow-jasper dreams
Have kindled her blue shade
(Or should a Naiad brush her cheek,
Perhaps a dream of jade!).

Turbid, the fountain says she wakes,
But if the waters meet
With singing, Naiads dance for her
On swallow-nimble feet.

The song was charming," said Chiron, "if overlong. Now may I have my beer? I will take it *instead* of the tea." Then he looked to the door. Marguerite and Oryx had entered the room. They paused, returned his gaze, and waited for him to speak.

"Ah," sighed Chiron. "The troublemakers. I thought I was rid of them once."

"Without them, I would be dead," said Silver Bells. "If they hadn't attracted the Sphinx—"

"I have brought some garlands," Melissa said. "First for Silver Bells because of our love for him. Then for Oryx because I love him best." Rare white violets for Silver Bells, richer yellow for Oryx. She had wrapped them in damp moss to protect the flowers.

"And I wore the moss like gloves. I never touched a petal. Wear them for luck," she said. "My two favorite men!" But she looked at Oryx with misty eyes. It was his sadness that he must grow and die; hers, that she could not grow and claim his desire. It was their gladness that they could love each other as friends. "I gathered the flowers myself, and butterflies flecked them with pollen dust. Only the white, of course. The others are gold already."

"Child," said Chiron. "Watch if you like, but make yourself scarce. Better, invisible. You might enjoy yourselves behind the screen. I have always said that children are meant to be seen—on occasion—but never to interrupt their king. Take Eunostos to play with you."

"I'm much too old to play," Eunostos announced. "I grew to a man, you see, when I went in search of my uncle. I have even captained a ship!"

"He did the work of a man," his uncle was quick to say. "And showed the courage too."

"At *eight?* Oh, very well. Stay if you must, Eunostos. But I fear you will miss the best of the conversation. That is to say, my aphorisms. I have a dozen poised on my tongue. Some are extremely profound, and not for a child's"—a warning look from Silver Bells—"a young man's ears. But now to our captives. Silver Bells, you ought to have let the Tritons dispose of them. Now I must plan their fate before I sup. I hate to think at such times. It gives me a stomach ache."

"Chiron," said Moschus. He was drunk of course, but he chose his words with care and spoke without a slur. "I am your first cousin once removed."

"True."

"And we sometimes drink together."

"True."

"And wench."

"Er, let us say that you help me to choose my wives."

"And concubines. And light o' loves. Well, I won't."

"Won't what?"

"Anything if you exile our Human friends. They aren't all bad, you know, those Humans we hate and mistrust. Just as the Beasts are not all good. They have their greedy merchants and heartless crowds. We have our Harpies and Tritons and Sphinxes."

"I'm proud of you, Moschus," I whispered. Why, he might have been sober, the eloquent Beast! "AND I" (a loud and commanding voice; being a queen had added command) "WILL NOT—EVER—ENTERTAIN A BEAST WHO EXILES MY FRIENDS, NOT EVEN A KING."

"Where is the beer?" sulked Chiron.

"We are waiting your judgment, of King of Kings," said Thyme, in a small but resolute voice. "Of course you may have some tea while you decide. Marjoram, pour a cup for our mightiest guest."

"Tea? Tea? Oh, very well. Let them stay. But forever, you understand. They can't change their minds and return to their peeople and tell."

"Why would we want to return?" smiled Marguerite. "I have forgotten my trade. I would have to marry a Cretan and wait on his ship. An Egyptian and wait on his caravan. An Achaean and see him carried home on a shield. And all the while, sit at a spinning wheel and think up tasks for my slaves."

"And I have forgotten to skulk," said Oryx. "Or hide. Or hit a man on the head. I am quite unsuited to life in the world at large. Can you see me as a gardener or a fisherman?"

"Besides," she concluded, "our friends are here."

"You will have to work," said Chiron. "Build your own house. Grow your own food"

"I'll help," I said "They can live in one of my trees until they have built their house."

"And I will teach them to garden," Eunostos said. "Radishes. Carrots. Everything they will need."

"And I. . . ."

"And I. . . ."

"Forever," smiled Silver Bells.

"But Humans die," said Melissa.

"All of us die," I said. "After awhile."

"But they die so quickly, don't they?"

"Time," said Marguerite, "is measured by deeds,

185

not years. If Oryx and I are happy half of the time, and never hopeless or bitter even the other half, why then our lives shall seem very long."

"Like Zoe's," Oryx said.

"Uncle," Eunostos asked. "Sing us one of your songs Or if you like, I could sing a song of my own. An epic about our battle with the Sphinx."

"Silver Bells is your elder," I interposed. "He shall sing first. Then, if we still have time, which I doubt—"

"On with the song!" (Rude little Girls to interrupt! And *me*, who had captained them on the Triton seas!)

"There's plenty of time," said Eunostos. "There always is at a Naiad party."

"On with the song," I cried.

And Silver Bells sang:

THE SNOW AND THE SEED

The snow brought slumber in his quiet hands
"Oblivion is kind," he said, "lie still."
The seed gave one sharp cry:
"Strange snow, I dread your chill!"
And ceased to grow.

But when rough spring had made his green
  demands
That buried life should labor into light
And supplicate the sky,
The seed remembered night
And thanked the snow.

186

CRY SILVER BELLS

Silver Bells started the song with his usual resonance but paused, it seemed to me, unduly long before he reached the conclusion. In fact, I feared that Eunostos might finish the song. But Silver Bells coughed and touched his throat and resumed in a softer voice, almost a whisper, like an echo from an empty, forgotten well. I was angry with spring; I disliked the snow; I pitied the reawakened seed.

"What's the point?" asked the king. "It isn't even raunchy. Bring on the beer!"

"It was much too sad for a party," I said. "What we need is a drinking song."

"But it *isn't* sad," Eunostos protested. "It's simply— true."

"Silver Bells had better have some tea," said Melissa. He looks—she groped for a gentle word— "tipsy."

"Tipsy or sick?" I demanded, taking a closer look at the russet skin which had faded to white.

"My uncle has *never* been drunk," Eunostos protested. "Except when Alyssum died. He must be sick."

Silver Bells swayed, clutched for support but, finding neither a couch nor a chair, lurched against a wall and subsided onto the floor. I was much too surprised to give him a hand. He was our pillar; he was our paragon. Had he not defeated the Sphinx?

"I need some air," he gasped. "The room is so hot. Especially around my neck." He tore the wreath from his throat. "Forgive me, Melissa. Forgive me, everyone. . . ."

(Forgive you? Forgive *me*, my dearest, for being

187

less than Alyssum! She would have known how to
medicine you.)

No, not even Alyssum. . . .

I do not remember how I ran from the room, stag-
gered out of the tunnel and into the dying light. . . .
I do not remember, except that I saw them with cruel
clarity: two butterflies, side by side on the ground between the dragon guards. I knew them behind their
disguise, Alyssum and her friend from the Cretan
arena. Sphinxes; yes, even Alyssum, the Lamia, who
had fooled the best of us; and both had come to destroy Silver Bells.

"No!" I cried.

But truth is a goddess who is inescapable. Words
were inadequate for her harsh demands. She paraded
pictures before my resistant mind. . . .

The Sphinxes learn from the Harpies of Silver
Bells, noblest of his race, nature's opposite to the worst
of their race: Alyssum. Intolerable! Alyssum, cany and
heartless, assumes a Naiad's shape and sails in the
Nilus to Crete. The Tritons guide her into our cove.
She pretends they have killed her crew. She is welcomed under the fountain—unlike a Sphinx, a Lamia
likes the water—and she wins the love of the forest
and Silver Bells. Why not become a Sphinx and kill
him at once? But the Beasts of the Country would
never let her escape. She has learned how to wait. She
has learned how to plot. Stealth allows her to practice
her guile. Remember, she is a Lamia, hater of men.

She will wed the Beast she intends to kill! How she intended to kill him, who can say? But a wife has a hundred ways, hemlock poured in the ear while her husband sleeps, a sudden fire, a fall, and she, the widow, she, the pitiless, wins the pity of unsuspecting friends.

Then, the unexpected. She strays to the edge of the forest, yearning perhaps for a desert, a lack of trees, a want of grass. She is caught in the gamemaster's net. She, not he, is the first to die. She returns as a butterfly to calculate ways to kill a Minotaur. The Harpies report the reversal to her people in Libya.

Another Sphinx arrives on the island, and not to search for Oryx and Marguerite. (They hid in a pool, remember, and masked their scent. They were never seen, they fled from a foe who never knew of them.) Silver Bells in the ring . . . a second Sphinx, a second chance. . . . Failing, evil dwindles into a butterfly.

She joins Alyssum in the Country to wait . . . to look for a way . . . to waylay a Bear Girl, plucking flowers for a wreath. They gather the Deadly Nightshade's slow-acting poison; dip their wings in its pollen —every part of the plant is lethal to Beasts, as to butterflies. They would surely have known that the yellow and rarer flowers were meant for Oryx, Melissa's favorite; the white for Silver Bells. Their bodies wither and die but a fatal wreath, in the paws of a little girl, is placed around Silver Bell's neck.

I studied them in the greenness of moss; their broken bodies and tattered wings. I started to grind them under my sandals' weight, but paused and watched them return to chrysalis, saffron muted to brown, hardened secretion, enclosing a pulpy core. In miniature, woman returning to Sphinx.

I ran, I ran. . . .

How many turns of the hour-glass did I stay in my father tree? I will never emerge, I thought. Here I am fathered, at least. Here I am shut from the smoke of the funeral pyre, the weeping of those who loved him, but not too deeply for tears.

But grief accepts no parents; she shuts you into a desert and hides the path to the trees. Gray sand, gray rocks . . . a sun which never sets, which burns instead of warms. What is the sound of surf in a secret cove? What is the color of a phoenix wing? What are the words of Silver Bells' song? "That buried life should labor into light." No, he was wrong! *If burning life could burrow into night . . . If burning life. . . .*

Kindly voices hailed me from the ground, Melissa, Moschus, Phlebas . . .

"Zoe, you must eat."

"Go away," I called. "Or bring me snow. You are speaking to the dead."

"You have a fever, Zoe. We have brought you a brew of Meadow-sweet and fennel. Oryx has taken a bowl to Marguerite."

"Ghosts cannot eat. Ghosts become butterflies."

I willed my arms to billow into wings and lift me from my house and dash the horror of me—shape of murderers, shape of death—against the grateful ground.

"Aunt Zoe."

"Go away."

"Aunt Zoe, it's Eunostos." The little boy in him had climbed my tree and wriggled through the window like a snake.

"I know who it is."

"May I hug you, Aunt Zoe?"

"Quickly, child." We were companions in a common grief. How could I wound him by refusing his hug?

"We love him, don't we?"

"You're all alone, now, aren't you, dear? You may come to live with me here in my tree. Give me a little time, though."

"Thank you, Aunt Zoe. I would like to live with you."

"Give me a little time. . . ."

"First," he persisted, "I have a gift for you."

"What, child?"

"Outside the tree."

"No! The winding stairs. . . ."

"Please. You needn't be afraid. Here. I'll steady you."

"Oh, very well."

"You brought me from my tree to see a *snake?*"

"Snakes are good luck."

"We have lost our luck, you and I."

"This one is special, I think."

Smooth, russet, agile, he raised his head and flicked his narrow tongue. I have no fear of snakes. Only the

191

Israelites, that curious desert tribe, dislike them because of an ancient tale. (Egyptians fear but also worship them.) For us a snake is fortune and fertility, perhaps a man's imperishable soul.

"A horned viper," I said. "Poison in Egypt. Harmless here on Crete."

"Now you must kneel."

"Kneel? My dear, I can hardly stand. If I kneel, I shall surely collapse."

"I'll steady you. There. Do you see?"

"His horns are like little antlers, aren't they? Is that what you meant me to see?"

"Bend your ear to him. What do you hear?"

"Hear? You sound as if you expect him to speak! Snakes don't talk, they hiss."

"Closer."

"Why, it sounds like tiny bells."

"Silver bells."

I felt a breeze in my face. I did not even need Eunostos' help to stand.

"I must see to our sick," I said. "After all, we run an Asklepion, don't we?"